I0763605

RATHGAR

TAYLOR NEPTUNE
JASPER THORNE

BIRTHDAY PARTY

JANIE

If someone had told me I would be spending my nineteenth birthday on an alien planet, I would have laughed in their face.

Oh, how times have changed.

My name's Janie. One year ago, my older sister Lara left Earth as part of an intergalactic surrogacy program. We were in dire straits at the time and needed the money, but it turned out to be so much more.

Now I'm sitting here with my sister, her alpha warlord husband, and their darling baby as we share a piece of strawberry cake. It's something our mom used to make us when we were kids. We had it every birthday, and even after our mom passed, Lara made sure to continue the tradition.

Even now that we're on a whole new planet, surrounded by aliens, she knows just how to make me smile. That's one of the many things I love about her.

I have to admit, I wasn't so sure about this alien breeding business at first. Getting paid to have babies for alien warriors sounded kind of shady, if you ask me. But then again, Iris's father ran off the moment I got the pregnancy test back. Guess I don't have the best experience with men, so it's hard for me to trust anyone.

Being a teen mom on a plague-ridden planet was hard enough. Losing our parents and then our jobs was even tougher. We were already having a tough time feeding ourselves before Iris came. Sometimes I lie awake at night and wonder what we would have done if Lara hadn't found the application for the Intergalactic Surrogacy Agency.

I shiver. Nothing good, that's for sure.

Iris squeals and reaches up to me, her chubby fingers flexing. Pulling off a soft piece of cake, I put it on her little fork and make zooming sounds toward her mouth.

"Here comes the spaceship…open wide!"

Iris opens her mouth and grabs the fork out of my hand, instead opting to smear the cake all over her cheeks with a laugh.

I can't help but snort. That's my girl. I used to say she was the messiest eater on planet Earth, but now she's giving even Aesirheim a run for its money. Speaking of Aesirheim...

It's so much like Earth in some ways, but in others…not at all. I can see why Lara fell in love with it, though. It's so lush, so exotic compared to the desolate, sun-cracked fields we left behind. Fantastical creatures beyond my wildest imaginations roam the landscape freely, giant mushroom forests loom over crystal-clear lakes, and the sunsets are — literally — out of this world.

I never thought I would have a chance to experience any of this. Thought my life was practically over when that scumbag knocked me up and ran off. I promised Lara and my baby that I would be there for them, be the best mother and sister I could be. I'd given up any hope of a happy ending for my own, but when Lara found hers, I wondered if maybe I was looking in all the wrong places.

"Happy Birthday, Janie." Lara raises a glass of the green, fizzy drink and clinks it against mine. "To a bright future, for all of us." There's a smile of pure contentment on my older sister's face.

"Cheers!"

"Cheers," I repeat, but my mind's elsewhere as I mull over all the changes that Lara's contract brought to our lives.

"You all right?" Lara nudges me. I don't bother trying to lie. She'll know anyway.

I give her a tight smile and take another sip of my drink. "I'm fine. Just thinking."

"About?" She raises a single eyebrow at me.

Because I can't lie to her, I can't meet her gaze. "The contract."

A pause. I'm staring at the ground, but even I can feel the tension in the air.

"You're not getting cold feet, are you?" Her voice is softer now. Worried. She knows what it would mean if I violated the contract. There's nothing really stopping them from tossing me back to my home planet if I don't fulfill the written terms.

"No, it's nothing like that." Is it? I worry that I was too hasty, but Iris and I didn't have many better alternatives.

"Are you still having side effects from the shot?"

I shake my head. "It was only a partial shot, remember? Just enough for Iris and I to adjust to the atmosphere on Aesirheim. The…" I swallow around the lump in my throat. "Real one comes after they find me a genetic match. Which should be any day now, now that I'm nineteen…"

"I know it's not the ideal solution, but that's the only way we were able to get you a visa." Soren, a huge golden-skinned alpha and my sister's husband, speaks up. "Believe me, I tried."

"I know. And I appreciate that. It's just a little nerve-wracking, is all." I try to brush the idea away like it's nothing, but it still sits heavy in my gut.

Lara takes my hand and squeezes it. "You'll be fine, sis. I promise. I mean, look how I turned out." She bounces Ray on her lap; Soren wraps a possessive arm around her waist. For a moment, my heart lurches. I could have had that.

I should have had that.

But it's fine. Really. I'm here now, with my sister and my daughter, and I have everything I could ask for. It's enough. Really. It's enough.

Until I crawl into an empty bed at night.

As I stare into my drink, I glance over at the sound of hoofbeats. The raiders are returning from their patrols, mounted upon huge beasts native to this planet. Their horns are longer and taller than my whole body, and the men astride them are even bigger still.

That's one thing about living on an alien planet: everything is so…big.

I've never been a tall woman, but being around the Aesir alphas makes me feel utterly tiny. They tower over us with their broad shoulders and bulging muscles. At least I know that if anything tries to attack, we'll be well protected.

I turn back to my drink and a spike of fear shoots up my throat. My little girl — my Iris — is gone.

Whirling around, I curse myself for taking my eyes off of her. I'd been too caught up in my own thoughts to notice. Where had she run off to?

And that's when I hear her signature laugh. She's toddling with joy straight toward the approaching raiders. They're disheveled, dirty, and caked with blood and dirt. That doesn't seem to stop her. With all the joyful innocence of a child, she stretches out her little arms and grabs on to the pant leg of the meanest, grumpiest looking warlord that I've ever seen.

Rathgar. Even the name scares me. He's one of the biggest of them all, always wearing a sour scowl that makes my skin crawl. Many of Soren's people have accepted us readily, but he always seems to look down his nose at me. Makes me feel unwanted. Small. Insignificant.

And now my little girl's tugging on his pant leg.

Ah, nuts. Happy birthday to me, I guess. I take a breath before walking towards them.

IRIS PLAYING

RATHGAR

I'll never understand the importance Earthlings place on birthdays. It's utterly foreign to me. Why celebrate the day of one's birth? It's the same as any other. We all age regardless. But — I've learned since Soren took on a human bride — they have celebrations and 'parties', as they call them, for all kinds of things.

Perhaps to give their pitifully short lifetimes meaning.

I've certainly stopped counting mine. It matters not, only that I'm in the prime of my life as a warrior for our planet. As Soren's second-in-command, I take care of the dirty work he doesn't want to, and that's fine with me. I have no desire to lead. He does a good enough job of that himself. For the most part, my status allows me to do whatever I want. Not many people can boss me around, and that suits me just fine.

Soren keeps going on about his human mate and the surrogacy agency our planet partnered with. Sure, it worked for him, but there's no guarantee lightning might strike twice, is there? I've never thought much about having a child, to be honest, but Soren says it will be good for the clan. It will set an example for others to follow. And who am I to reject my commander's wishes?

The last thing I want to do when returning from a raid, bloodied but successful, is to attend one of these human celebrations. It's a favor to my commander, nothing more.

At least, until I feel a small hand tugging at the hem of my pants. I look down, my blood high and still ready to strike, and see the smallest little thing.

A tiny human looks up at me, blissfully ignorant of how dangerous I am. How many lives I've taken. In fact, she looks almost…happy? Small fingers tug at my leg and reach up toward me like she's expecting something. Her soft mouth opens and the strangest, high pitched sound comes out. Laughter? At me?

It's all kinds of confusing. What is she doing here? Where is her mother? No Aesir parent worth their salt would leave a little one unattended. Is this something else the Earthlings do differently? No sooner do I think that than I hear panicked footsteps. A woman rushes toward me and swoops the tiny human away before muttering stammered apologies.

She doesn't meet my eyes, all bowed posture, dark hair, and soft skin. She's the first human I've met besides Soren's mate Lara. Wasn't this one supposed to be her younger sister or something? I can see the resemblance now that I look a bit closer. They both hold a certain sort of beauty, I'll admit. Different than the Aesir women, to be sure, but enthralling in their own way. I can see why Soren fell for his woman, but his utter near-addiction to her doesn't make any sense.

Maybe it's due to that omega thing Soren told us about. As the ruling warlords of Aesirheim, we underwent genetic modifications in order to boost our strength and power. They called us 'alphas'. It allowed us to finally take back our homeland, but it unfortunately affected our ability to produce offspring.

The Intergalactic Surrogacy Agency matches people like us with volunteers called 'omegas' and ensures a healthy pregnancy. To someone like Soren it mattered a great deal — the high warlord needed to produce heirs and keep his line strong.

As for me? I didn't think about it too much.

But as I look upon this small human and her child, I can't deny there's something intriguing about her. She carries a faint floral scent, too soft and feminine for the hard landscapes of Aesirheim. It's utterly unfamiliar, and yet…my heart stutters a bit in my chest. My mouth dries. I want to know more, and that scares me.

"—so sorry, it won't happen again, I'll get out of your hair—"

Her words catch up to me, soft and pleading. I scowl — why does she still not meet my gaze? Does she not know it's common respect? Does she not care?

"You, human woman." The words come out harsher than I intend. She freezes, tensing, like a cornered animal about to run. "What do you think you're doing, letting your offspring run free like that?" I cross my arms. "Something could happen to them."

"I'm sorry, sir, she simply got away from me, it was only a few seconds and—"

"Don't apologize to me. Apologize to your girl. She's lucky she only found me and not one of our enemies. Or don't you know what they do to children out there?" It's for her own good. I'm not trying to be cruel, but she needs to know she's not on Earth anymore. There's a reason we fight as hard as we do. The world can be an unkind, dangerous place — especially for children. Why doesn't she know that? Why doesn't she seem to care?

The woman holds her child closer to her chest. She lets out an angry huff and finally cranes her head up to meet my eyes. How cute — this weak-willed human thinks she can challenge me. "I said I'm sorry. I don't know how you take care of children here and I don't care. But last time I checked, you're not her father, so leave me alone. I won't bother you again." With a 'hmph', she turns on her heel and storms away, leaving me open-mouthed in the dust.

What just happened? And why did her fury ignite something inside me?

Maybe humans aren't so dull after all. I almost smile.

HUG

JANIE

He had some nerve, telling me how to mother my own child when all he does is fight all day. There's more to life than violence and glowering, not that he knows that or cares. I'm just grateful Lara's husband Soren doesn't treat her like that. I'd be having words with him if he did, and I would never have signed off on moving our entire family to this planet, food or no food.

I'm still thinking about our clash the next day while I'm at Lara and Soren's place. Today's the day I head off to the center, and to be honest, I'm kind of terrified. Not that I can show it. I have people counting on me here. Not least of all, Iris.

I know Lara will take good care of her, but I'm still nervous. What if they can't find a match for me? What if he turns out to be mean and nasty like Rathgar — or worse? There are too many variables, but there's nothing I can do now. It's either successfully complete this surrogacy program or get shipped off back to Earth. And with Lara and Ray living on this planet, that's out of the question.

Lara took a stand and put her fears aside to build a better life for us when she signed that contract. Now it's time for me to do the same.

I walk back to the bathroom to check on Iris — I'm trying and mostly failing to potty train her — and instead see a bare butt sticking out of the cabinet under the sink.

So much for that idea.

She's bent over, butt out, and when I crouch down to help her, she's fast asleep on the pile of towels there. I cover my mouth against a surprised laugh — why does she have to be so *cute*? Poor thing must be exhausted. I pull her into my arms and close the cabinet, reminding myself to child-proof the doors for next time. She wakes up on my shoulder and nuzzles into my neck.

I know she won't be this little forever, but I live for these moments. She's a handful on the best of days, but she's *my* handful. My Iris. And I don't know what I'd do without her.

"Mommy," she whines when I put her back into her bed. "I don't wanna."

"Aren't you tired? You fell asleep when going potty."

"I don't wanna."

She's lucky she's so cute. "All right, we'll go back into the living room. But if you fall asleep again, it's back to bed with you."

"Okay."

Shaking my head, I lead her back into the living room and pull out the blocks we were playing with earlier.

They're soft foam shapes of all different colors. Iris loves stacking them up into wobbly piles which are inherently structurally unsound. She then screams with laughter when they topple over. It's adorable, if a little loud.

Soren and Lara should be back any moment. They're out with their child Ray for the morning, and when they come back I'm handing off Iris while I head over to the ISA center to uphold my end of the contract that will ensure that Iris and I can stay here. I gulp, watching Iris stack the blocks again and again. She's so blissfully ignorant of what is to come. Little does she know her mommy's about to go get knocked up by an alien.

The door opens and I turn around, expecting Soren and Lara. Instead, it's the last person I want to see.

Rathgar looms in the doorway, all cold stares and tough muscles. The light catches the angles of his face and gleams on his gold skin.

I gasp despite myself, and my heart skips a beat or two. *He'd be hot, if he weren't such an asshole.* The thought comes unbidden — where did that come from? Sure, he had a handsome, dominant aura about him. All the alphas did. But that didn't mean I had to like it.

Besides, I've already been there, done that. I even have a kid to prove it.

He'd been nothing but rude to me ever since we met; I wasn't about to start changing my tune now.

"Where's Soren?" His eyes sweep the room and land on me. "I need to talk to him."

"Oh, he's not here right now. Him, Lara, and Ray are out for the morning. They should be back any minute, though. You can come back later?" I end on a hopeful note, praying he gets the hint.

He doesn't.

"I'll wait." He invites himself inside and stoops through the doorway, moving to stand against the wall in the living room. He crosses his arms and just stands there, glowering. He's so tall he nearly hits the ceiling, and Iris stops playing to look up at him.

“Why don’t you say hello, Iris?” I’m talking more out of nervousness at the moment. Anything to fill the empty air. I can’t stand him just hovering there. It gives me the creeps. Feels like he’s just waiting for me to mess up again so he can lecture me about what a bad mother I am.

I scowl at the thought. He doesn’t know a thing about me. It can stay that way for all I care.

Iris stares up at him with wide eyes for another few seconds before waving her small hand at him. She’s all but forgotten the blocks, her mouth hanging open in what looks like awe.

I don't get it. She's been around Soren plenty of times and never had this reaction.

"Hello." She says cheerfully before standing up on wobbly legs. Iris grasps the edge of the couch for support. "Hello." She says again.

I look over to Rathgar expectantly. Surely he's not so rude to ignore a child? But he simply stands there, having some sort of weird staring match with my daughter.

"Hello?" Iris says one more time, raising her hand. Her soft, sweet face pleads with him, yet he still does nothing.

Rathgar doesn't uncross his arms. He simply looks confused, his brow furrowed.

I fight the urge to roll my eyes. Not only is he a judgmental asshole, but he won't even be nice to my daughter. I'm about to ask him to leave when Iris starts wailing.

Hmph. Serves him right. She clearly said hello, and all he did was glare at her. No wonder she was scared! Rathgar's expression changes, but he looks even more unsettled than before, if that's even possible.

I don't want to curse him out in front of my daughter, so I give him the most furious glare I can before rushing to Iris's side. Pulling her into my arms, I try shushing her, but she's still sniffling and wailing. I pick her up off of the ground and kiss her cheek.

"Shh, you're all right. You're okay. Mommy's here."

Iris sniffs again and cranes her neck to look back at Rathgar. I thought she was scared of him, but she reaches out her hand again. "Hug."

Her sudden request catches me off guard. Had I heard that right? "You want a hug…from him?"

She reaches out again. "Hug."

I glance up at him, lips pulled into a smirk as I look at the expression on his face. What's Mr. Tall, Dark, and Dangerous going to do now? For such a fearsome warrior, he looks almost… scared. Over this little thing?

"You heard her," I taunt him. "Iris wants a hug. You're not really going to turn her down, are you? You're the one who gave me a lecture on taking care of kis."

Rathgar sputters. He flinches, eyeing the door. Looks like he's about to make a run for it. "A-are you sure?"

"Hug!" Iris spouts again. I raise my eyebrows at him, waiting to see how he responds.

Your move, big guy.

He freezes for a moment longer, looking for all the world like trapped prey even though he's normally a huge predator. I almost want to laugh, it's such a ridiculous juxtaposition. But then he swallows, gives a short nod, and holds out his arms. "All right. I will give her this…hug."

I hand Iris over and the moment she's in his arms, she quiets down. It's like magic. I can't believe it.

Rathgar's posture is stiff, his movements tense and unsure, but Iris looks so small in his huge arms. Almost like she's a newborn all over again. His face softens from its usual disdainful scowl and turns into something almost pleasant.

My heart takes notice, thudding in my chest as I watch this big man gently hold my daughter. He's so grumpy all the time and only seems to care about fighting. Yet with Iris in his arms he looks somehow at peace.

The sound of the door shakes me out of my thoughts. Lara, Soren, and Ray are back at last. Soren cocks his head when he sees Rathgar standing there with Iris. He flicks his gaze over to me, and then he swings his gaze back to Rathgar.

"Is everything all right?" Soren slips back into commander mode, straightening his posture.

I've never seen an alien blush before, but the look on Rathgar's face just about does it. He awkwardly hands Iris back to me before standing straight and giving him a traditional Aesir salute. "I came to inform you of my planned absence. I'm heading to the center later today and I wanted to make sure there was nothing else you needed of me before then."

My heart skips a beat. The center. There's only one place he could mean.

The Intergalactic Surrogacy Agency? Him?

Surely not…

"You're free to go." Soren nods, but I can tell he wants to say something else. "…Good luck."

Rathgar bows his head. "Thank you, commander."

"Wait," Lara cuts in. She glances from me to him, her lips creeping up into a scheming smile. I know that look. "Isn't your appointment today too, Janie?"

So much for keeping things low-key. "Yeah," I mumble. "You'll be able to look after Iris, right?"

"You know I'm happy to. It's no problem at all. And Ray will be overjoyed to have another little one to play with." She waves me toward the door. "Go on, take as long as you need."

"Hmm." Soren rumbles something deep in his chest, brow furrowed. I can practically see the gears turning in his head. "I was planning to escort Janie to the center myself, but if you have your appointments at the same time…"

Please don't say it. Please don't say it.

"Perhaps you could go together."

The air whooshes out of my lungs. There it was. I couldn't possibly handle traveling with this big brute. We were too different. He made sure I well knew what he thought of me, and I didn't want anything to do with him. This could only spell disaster.

Or at best, extreme discomfort.

I open my mouth to protest but Rathgar reacts quicker than I can. "Of course. I'll make sure nothing happens to her."

He looks over to me, extending his arm in a surprisingly friendly gesture. "Shall we?"

Yup. I'm totally screwed already. And I haven't even made it to the center yet.

HOPEFUL

JANIE

If I already had the omega serum running through my veins, there would be a lot better explanation for this.

But I'm sober as can be, and the thought of that big, mean alien warlord holding my baby girl just about has my ovaries exploding.

I huff out a breath and try to focus on the scenery. The checklist of things I'll need before moving into the cottages. Anything but him.

When Iris's father left us, I made things work. Lara and I became closer than ever, and we worked our butts off to provide Iris with the best life we could. I had always dreamed of having a large family, but that dream died the day he left. I vowed that I'd never rely on a man again. That I would make it where so many others had failed. That I would be the best darn single mother that I could.

That was before the ISA. That was before my sister found her soulmate in a gruff alien warlord. And that was before I agreed to do the same thing. For Iris's sake.

Now I'm astride this huge elk-like creature they call an aki, and I'm seated way too close to the growliest alien of them all. The size difference isn't lost on me — Rathgar's huge form dwarfs mine, especially with my back pressed up against his chest. One wide hand, large enough to cover my entire stomach, holds the reins while the other ghosts over my hip to stabilize me.

He shouldn't feel so hot and warm and vital against me. The steady rocking movement of the beast beneath us shouldn't rub against my privates and make the thoughts even harder to ignore. But it does, and all I can do now is pray he can't smell me and hope for a short trip.

Lara told me as much as she could about the process before I left. She explained the side effects and how sensitive she got when under the influence of the omega hormones. She also explained how…ahem…needy the alphas get when they smell their mate.

It would be a lie to say I'm not nervous. I can handle myself just fine, but if I want to stay on this planet with Lara I have to 'contribute'. I just hope it's worth it, and I'll have a miraculously wonderful experience just like Lara did.

I don't want to think about the alternative.

The whole notion of being in 'heat' terrifies me. I mean, I remember being a young horny teenager. I jumped into bed with a man who promised me the world and delivered nothing. All because I trusted him and his honeyed words. I can't go through that again. My heart can't take it.

So as long as I treat this as simply business, simply a due to be paid, I'll be fine. I'll make it through and I'll go back to my life like nothing ever happened.

No pressure.

Unable to handle the nervous silence any longer, I start talking, hoping that we can change the subject to something lighter. I fill the air with light chatter. Not that Rathgar's a very good conversationalist, but what can I say? I talk when I'm nervous.

"I never expected...well, I didn't know what to expect when Lara signed up for the program. She did it for me, you know. For Iris, really, and also my sake."

Rathgar's silent a moment, and I worry for a panicked second that he's going to ignore me just like he did back at Lara's place. Then he speaks. "So why are you here?"

That's a loaded question if I've ever heard one. I chew my lip, trying to think of how to say it. "Well, I love kids. I agreed to the program because I want to be able to stay here on this planet with Lara and Ray. I don't want to go back to Earth. There's nothing for me there if Lara wants to build her family here, and I'm grateful that we'll have food." I shake my head, grief already clenching at my gut. "But I'm not going to let my heart go so easily."

A few moments of silence pass between us, but then Rathgar surprises me with the change of topic. "Where is the girl's father? Did he fall in battle?"

Hmph. Of course he would think that. The reality is much more embarrassing. Already I'm kicking myself, not wanting to admit to my shame — my failure. But I was the one that started this, after all. To stop now would only give him more reasons to look down on me. I take a deep breath and shake my head. "No, nothing like that."

"Then what?"

The words feel like sandpaper in my mouth, but I force them out. "He, um...he left us. Didn't want to raise a child. He left as soon as I found out I was pregnant."

He pulls the aki to a dead stop, his reaction immediate. I feel every muscle tense in his body behind me. Can practically see the anger radiating off of his skin. Oh no. I've done it this time. I should have kept my big mouth shut…

"Shameful." The word comes out forced, through gritted teeth.

Yeah, I know. I want to curl into myself, to hop down off this huge beast and run back to my sister. Rathgar is telling me what everyone around us said when they realized that I was going to be a single mom. I want to forget this ever happened.

"He is no man."

Wait, huh?

The air simmers with tension. I dare not turn to face him. The sight of his displeased face would be too much to bear.

"To leave a child...to abdicate such responsibility like that..." His voice is low, lower than I've ever heard it. Laced with malice. "Such deeds would be punished by death among my kin."

With a jolt, we start moving again, and I see the buildings of the center come into view. "No Aesir man will ever abandon a woman or child in need. I promise you that."

I've heard that promise before. Why does Rathgar's promise give me hope when I shouldn't have any? Shouldn't I be smarter than that?

DIVINE JOKE

RATHGAR

Janie and I go our separate ways once we reach the center. I performed my duty and delivered her safely. That's all it was.

I won't think about the way she felt so soft beneath my touch or the way she swayed on Kestyra, my aki, as we rode toward the center. That way lies madness.

While the medical staff poke and prod at my body, my blood still boils at the thought of Janie's plight. Children were irreplaceable miracles here on Aesirheim. They were so few and far between, so hard to conceive and carry to term, that the thought of someone abandoning Janie and her baby like that…

It makes me want to hurt something. Preferably the lowlife that made her feel this way.

She's maddening and far too talkative, but she deserves better. Even I know that. And there's one thing we can both agree on: we're both doing this out of duty. Out of obligation. We have no desire to put our hearts on the line.

As for me? I'm only following orders. Soren practically threatened me with exile if I didn't. Good for him that he found his heart-mate and all, but I'm not sure I believe in that stuff. And even if I did, I don't think a long-term relationship like that is right for me anyway. What kind of woman would love a hardened warrior like me?

I don't have Soren's charm, nor do I have his position or influence. I may be second in command, but at the end of the day, I'm just a soldier. I've spent my whole life on the battlefield. I don't know anything else. Especially not when it comes to relationships.

I barely understand my fellow clan members. How am I going to be able to relate to someone from a totally different planet?

The waiting room is too small. Too claustrophobic. I get up and stretch my legs, deciding to walk around and explore while I wait for the test results to come back. It's all a very complicated process that I only half-listened to, but apparently they took my DNA and used it to cross-check with all the other humans in their database.

Once they find a genetic match who will be able to bear my offspring, they'll call us in and we'll be off to the cottages. One quick screw, I'll get her knocked up, and I'll provide everything the baby and mother needs to survive and thrive. I'll get my reward, and our population will swell once more. It's a win-win.

Right?

I groan, running a hand through my hair and over my braid. None of this would have happened if it weren't for the Alpha experiment. Things were different back then. Our people were plentiful and prosperous, spreading across the globe and across the galaxy. It seemed nothing could get in our way…

Until the war.

We fought off foe after foe, each tougher and meaner than the rest. The death toll grew, and still they came. We couldn't beat them with numbers or firepower. We just didn't have what it took. What we needed was an edge. A competitive advantage.

And so the Alpha experiment was born. Scientists worked in secret to develop a drug that would alter our bodily chemistry and make us stronger, faster, smarter. They molded us into the perfect soldiers and at long last, we turned the tide of battle. We were finally at peace.

But at what cost?

Plummeting birth rates put us in danger all over again, and that's where the Intergalactic Surrogacy Agency came in. That's all it was. A business transaction.

Now if only my cock would remember that…

The center's larger than I thought it would be. Long hallways of rooms shoot off from a central lobby where everyone checks in. There are about a half dozen women there in the waiting room, all with varying looks of nervousness or anticipation.

I notice their scents, but only barely. Humans smell so differently, but it's not unwelcome. Then again, it's nothing like Soren described, either.

The way he told it, the first scent he caught of Lara practically knocked the wind out of him. Wiped every thought out of his mind. Sent him into some kind of frenzy, tearing through the crowd just to find her.

Yeah, not for me. They smell nice and all. But nothing stands out. A pretty floral scent here. A citrusy scent there. One that reminds me of mint tea catches my attention for a fraction of a second, but the scent fades away just as easily.

I shrug and try another hallway. Maybe they won't find a match for me, after all. Maybe I'm just too incompatible. Too brutish even for their high-tech matching system. Wouldn't surprise me.

I turn another corner, grumbling. Might as well go back to the main lobby. Maybe they'll let me leave and come back once the tests are done. I hate sitting around in one place for too long. I need to be up and moving, not sitting in these tiny chairs in these tiny, sterile rooms.

The sooner this is over with, the better.

And that's when it hits me.

It takes a moment to register, at first. It's not so different from all the other scents flying around. But with each step I take, it grows stronger.

It's…familiar, somehow. I can't put a finger on it. Fresh grass and sunshine and rain. But better. So much better.

Was this…?

My heart skips a beat. Blood rushes to my head first. The room spins. My senses go into overdrive. What *was* that? And where was it coming from?

Then the blood rushes to my *other* head, and all bets are off.

It's her. It has to be. It's her.

My legs start moving before my thoughts can catch up. I'm sprinting down the hall like a man possessed. My mouth waters. My cock aches.

Every cell in my body tingles with sensation. With triumph.

It's close to the high I get from battle, but even that's not enough. It's more. So much more.

Blood roars in my ears. My heart thuds out a heavy rhythm. I'm practically panting as I round the corner and see the door at the end of the hall. There.

Putting on a burst of speed, I smash into the door and burst in without even thinking of the consequences. All I know is that my body *needs* to know who that delicious fragrance belongs to.

So imagine my surprise when I see a very startled Janie sitting there on the examination table.

She screams, and that's when my brain makes the connection.

My match — my omega — is her.

The gods are really having a laugh at me this time.

THIGH ACHE

JANIE

I know that Lara warned me about the side effects before I signed the contract, but nothing could have prepared me for this. Since Iris and I already had partial inoculations, they told me that the omega hormones in the shot would take effect much faster.

I didn't think they meant literal minutes.

It came on like a tidal wave, nearly knocking the wind right out of me. Everything was…hot. But it was more than that. I squirmed on the table while Orvox ran a set of routine tests. I wish she'd hurry up.

My body aches, itches, and burns all at the same time. The closest thing I can compare it to was when I ran a really high fever as a child. But even that's not enough. I need…something.

My brain's still racing to catch up, but I have a feeling I know just what that something is.

No turning back now.

I squeeze my thighs together and try to quell the ache. The overhead lights are too bright. The sounds too loud. My skin pricks with gooseflesh. I don't know what I need but I know I need out of here, now.

"Are we done?" I ask Orvox breathlessly. She doesn't seem deterred by my condition. Guess she's seen it all before.

"Just about," she tells me. "Your body is reacting more quickly than than the others'." She looks up from her tablet. I'm worried at the cool tone of her voice.

"Is that bad?" My voice catches in my throat. Am I going to get kicked off the planet with Iris because I'm defective? What if they can't find any suitable genetic matches for me among the alien warriors? Soren would try to stop it, I'm sure, but I am unsure if he'd be able to.

"No, it's not bad. It's likely due to your unique situation, and once I get the test results back you'll be escorted to the cottages for the duration of your stay."

My heart thuds painfully. The cottages. She makes it sound so idyllic. And they are luxurious, according to Lara, but that doesn't change what they are.

Breeding prisons.

Another wave hits me and I suck in a breath despite myself, grabbing onto the edges of the table for support. It's been a while since I had enough me time to even think about sex, but I've never felt like this before. Not even when I was super horny during my pregnancy.

This is like an all-consuming inferno, threatening to burn me from this inside out.

“Are you sure this is normal?” I squirm in my seat, breaths starting to turn into labored pants. “I feel…”

“Not to worry.” Orvox’s voice is calm, self assured. It’s her kindly tone that I cling on to with the rest of my sanity. She wouldn’t let anything happen to me. “This kind of reaction is not dangerous. It’s come on quicker than usual, but it just means your body is ready to carry a baby.”

My stomach clenches. Yeah. The whole reason I’m here.

The door bangs open and I’m so startled, so over-sensitive that I draw my legs up to my chest and scream. My second reaction?

Seeing Rathgar's hulking silhouette looming in the doorway, looking almost as crazed as I am.

Oh, you have *got* to be kidding me.

My head pounds. My veins pulse with need and my breaths come in short gasps. I need to get out of here. Need to find a place where I can be alone, where I can get some relief…

But my relief is standing right there in the doorway. The last man I would have expected, and the last man I wanted to see right now. I should be running away as fast as my legs will take me, but I'm rooted to the spot.

It can't be him. Anyone but him.

But as my eyes take in his wide frame and drop lower to the impressive bulge in his trousers, it's all I can do to keep from throwing myself at him.

Orvox moves quick, quicker than I've seen any alien move. She stands between us, unafraid of the snarling alpha. She's braver than I am, then.

"What is the meaning of this?" She spits at him. "This is a private room."

Rathgar *growls* with such a timbre it vibrates through my bones. "And she's mine." He's looking past Orvox's spindly frame. Eyes, lit with unquenchable passion and sheer rage, take in every curve of my body.

"The tests aren't even done yet—" Orvox says, standing her ground. "You'll have to go back to the waiting room like everyone else, or you'll be out of the program for good." She glares up at him, and I marvel at how she can be so fierce in the face of these dangerous alpha warriors. "You've done enough to void your contract here and now, but I'll give you one more chance. Leave at once."

Rathgar grunts, his eyes never leaving mine. "Check your tablet. Check your fancy tests and data. You'll see that I'm right." His hands clench into fists at his side. I curl into myself further, but the side of his raw power only sends another wave of pleasure and need coursing through me.

Is he about to start throwing punches? He wouldn't dare, right?

They face off for another few tense seconds, then she takes the tablet and makes a big show of tapping through the test results. Her mouth drops open. She looks up to Rathgar, then back to me. "Impossible."

Rathgar crosses his arms. "You see? I'm right."

I can't hold my silence any longer. They're standing here fighting over me like I'm some prize to be won, not a living, breathing, human being. "Um, hello." I wave at them. "Right here."

Orvox turns to me, her icy expression melting instantly back into the doting caretaker. "He's correct," she says at last. "You can see for yourself." Orvox flicks through a few screens and holds the tablet in front of my face, but all I see is a bunch of graphs and labels in a foreign language. I have no idea how to read it.

"There's got to be a mistake or something, right?" I know it's not likely, but it's my last chance not to be stuck with *him* for the next year. "Something you read or interpreted wrong?"

Rathgar's still standing there, glowering past Orvox at me. She's the only thing between us. She's the only thing keeping him from pouncing, and for a split second of insanity, I almost wish he would.

"I'm sorry, Miss Michaels. The data doesn't lie. Based on the available candidates in our database, Rathgar's genetic material forms the closest match with your own. You've also been matched based on psychographic factors as well."

The words run together in my head. I'm not really listening to the details — all I'm hearing is that this is it.

This growly, mean brute of an alpha is my assigned mate. And I've never wanted anyone so badly in my life.

Heaven help me.

If he thinks I'm going to stand down and be his pretty little omega, he's got another thing coming. I cross my arms and stare at him, trying to match his ferocity and failing.

“Well. You heard her.” I jut my chin upward in challenge. My body aches in a way I never knew possible. Conflicting thoughts war in my head.

I hate him. I want to tear his clothes off. He’s an asshole. I want to feel his arms around me. He’s the last man on Aesirheim I’d want to mate with. I want his thick cock filling me deep, satisfying an itch I never knew I had…

My face flushes, but I stand firm. Rathgar stares back at me, teeth bared into a snarl.

“Orvox,” I snap at the woman standing between us. “Show me where the cottages are. We have some business to attend to.” I pause on the word ‘business’, making sure he sees me say it.

Rathgar takes a step toward me. "Now wait just a minute—"

I know I shouldn't, but my blood's already hot and my filter's totally gone. "What's the matter? Scared?" I snort. "Either be an alpha and get us out of here, or I'll find someone who will."

Everything happens so fast after that. The tension in the air snaps like a gunshot and Rathgar lunges for me, sidestepping Orvox just in time. His thick golden arms wrap around my waist and with a shriek, I'm in the air.

He holds me like I weigh nothing. Like I'm nothing more than cargo. Draped over his shoulder like a sack of potatoes, he snarls at Orvox in their language until she hands him a keycard.

With that in hand, the doors swish open once more.

The ground jolts and twists. Everything's upside down, and from this vantage all I can see is the muscled planes of his back working with every long stride. That, and the taut, shapely curve of his ass.

I should feel ashamed, humiliated. Being slung over this big brute's shoulder and taken like an animal. But despite all logic, his rough treatment only turns me on more. My skin tingles at his touch, and all I can think as he bodily carries me out of the center is that I want *more*.

SLICK SPANKING

RATHGAR

How *dare* Janie. She comes to *my* planet and starts to make comments about *my* status? If she were anyone else, I'd have her head. But somehow, her feistiness stirs a fire inside me I'd long forgotten.

It's similar to the thrill of battle, but warmer. More intimate. My heart beats in time with each twitch of my hardening cock as I sling her over my shoulder. Gods, she's so tiny. I can carry her with one arm, no problem.

She's screaming and flailing and kicking. It's cute, actually. That she thinks she actually has a chance against me.

Be an alpha and get us out of here, or I'll find someone who will.

The words ring in my head as I take sure, ample strides out of the center and back to the hitching post. People stare and whisper as we pass, but I pay them no mind.

Let them.

If she's to be my assigned partner, then we'll get it over with as soon as possible. That way we won't have to spend more time together than necessary.

At least, that's what my rational brain tries to tell myself. Part of me still yells that she's insufferable. Loud. Too careless and too curious for her own good.

But another part — a growing part — wants to see her naked and bound to my bed. Wants to feel her soft flesh beneath my fingertips, and wants to hear her screams of pleasure as she comes undone around me.

I'll show her what an alpha really is. Make sure she never forgets it. And by the time I'm done, no other alpha will ever try to take what's mine again.

The landscape blurs around us. I'm holding Janie possessively against my torso as we ride. Her scent fills every sense I have. Intoxicating. Addicting. Overwhelming. Now I know what

Soren was talking about. Is it like this with every omega, I wonder?

Or just her?

The thought crops up for a fraction of a second, but I brush it away. She's nothing more than a means to an end. I didn't come here to give my heart away, and neither did she.

I just hope my body can remember what my brain wants.

WE REACH the cottages in record time. By the time I help her down, she's squirming and panting against me. Her scent grows with each passing moment. Her bravado rears its head every now and then, as if she remembered she was supposed to resist, but she's powerless against the pull of the omega serum.

That makes two of us.

When I get her back on the ground, she sags against me, legs wobbling from the ride. "Rathgar…" She all but moans, looking up at me with those perfect lips just slightly parted. "You're…"

I sweep her up into a bridal carry and relish the way she yelps with surprise. From this angle I can feel the soft curves of her body against me. I can see her flushed face and the emotions she's trying so hard to hide. But most of all, I can see the damp spot between her legs where slick had already soaked through the fabric.

Fuck, I need to get her inside before I mount her right here.

Good thing I learned how to multi-task in the service, because I'm swiping open the security panel with one hand while holding Janie close with the other. In a matter of seconds we're inside — far too long, if you ask me — and I waste no time heading straight for the bedroom.

She deserves better than this. She deserves a good, proper mating ritual. I know what a heart-mate would be owed, and Soren and Lara are lucky to have what they do. But that's not what Janie is going to get. Not tonight.

Janie questioned not only me, but my status as an alpha, and it doesn't matter who she is. I won't let that stand.

Soren always reminds me that Earth girls are different than us. They have different beliefs and customs. They come from a whole different planet. But right now, that doesn't matter. What does matter is that she's here on my turf and she's breaking my rules.

"Where are you—" Janie's voice is weak, trembling against my chest. She's looking around the huge cottage in awe, but there's only one place I want to be right now — balls deep in her delicious pussy.

"Welcome home." I lay her down on the bed, delighting in the silhouette before sitting down beside her. She's so perfect in this moment. So tender, with her heaving breasts and her soft flesh just begging to be worshiped.

But first, there's something I need to do.

Sitting on the edge of the bed, I pull her to me until she's draped over my lap, ass high in the air. My cock jumps at the contact, straining against my trousers and leaving a spot of wetness behind. Janie squeaks and tries to get up again, but I put a hand on the back of her neck and hold her down.

"Stay." The word tingles on my tongue, some hidden power laced behind the seemingly simple words. She stops immediately, growing pliant to my touch. Janie tilts her head, just enough to catch my eye.

She's still talking, but her voice no longer has that rebellious edge to it. It's tinged with desire, whispery and a little hoarse. "W-what are you doing?" She stammers. "I thought we were gonna..."

"We are." I slip a hand down her back until it comes to rest on the full swell of her ass. "But first, there's a little disciplinary problem we need to address."

"Wait, wha—" Her voice cuts off in the cutest little squeak as I smack her ass. I rub the soft curve there, digging my fingers in. For such a small being, she has such a voluptuous body. I can't get enough of.

Neither can my cock, apparently, because it aches and twitches upward, trying to find its mark. Not yet, though.

Not until she comes apart in my arms, begging for what I'm about to do to her.

Janie freezes over my lap. She stops wriggling, but her shoulders rise and fall with quick, shuddered breaths. I reach down and push her hair to one side. She breaks out in goosebumps at my mere touch. With a gasp, she pushes her upward into my hand, looking for something more.

And who am I to deny such a beautiful creature? I wrap one hand around her ponytail and hold it taut while spanking her again with the other. Her cries light up the room, anguish and arousal all rolled into one.

It's maddening. It's addicting.

It's perfect.

"I know you think you can waltz in here and do whatever you like," I growl as I give her another spank. "I know you think that contract protects you." Spank. "But you're forgetting one thing."

Janie doesn't answer. All I hear are her panted breaths. All I can smell is the hot, wet musk of her arousal.

I give her ponytail a tug, and she arches upward with a cry.

"Answer me."

"What?" Janie pants. Her eyes hang half-closed, lidded with desire.

So this is the heat that Soren warned me about. This is the optimal window for breeding, and I'm going to fill her up as many times as it takes until she's round with my child.

"What you're forgetting," I start, letting up on the ponytail so her head droops lower. Lucky for me, the change in her center of gravity also means her ass lifts further toward my hand. "Is that while you're on this planet, while you're under this contract, you're mine." I rain another slap on her ass and when she wails this time, it's no longer laced with pain.

It's almost…a moan? Did I really hear that right?

I massage the fleshy globes, one and then the other. She's practically bucking up into my hand, which turns me on far more than it should.

This was supposed to be her punishment. So why does it feel like the tables have turned?

Seeing her here like this, quaking and moaning at something that, by all accounts, shouldn't have been enjoyable, lights me up with a more feral passion than I've ever felt.

I remember how confused, but how aroused, I was when she talked back to me the first time. None of the Aesir women wanted to try their luck with such a high-ranking official. They knew our ways and customs too well to break them.

But Janie…she's different. She doesn't know any better, and while it's maddening on the best of days, it's also something else.

Really fucking sexy.

It's taking all I have not to forget the spanking entirely, throw her over on the bed and plunge my cock in her wet heat as deep as it will go. I've trained far harder than this. Have faced far more dastardly enemies, leaving my life and the lives of my people on the line.

So why was this more of a challenge than all of them?

I've only been spanking over her skirt until now, but I can't wait any longer. I need to know what's underneath. With a grunt, I push her skirt up and over her waist, sucking in a breath when I find she's not wearing any panties.

Damn, this girl is going to be the end of me.

It's no wonder now why she was leaking slick everywhere. No wonder why I could smell her so strongly. Why her need wrapped around me like chains, threatening to squeeze the very life from my lungs.

"You did this on purpose," I growl. I pull on her ponytail till her head tilts up and toward me. "Didn't you?"

Her whole face is red, all the way up to her ears. She makes a little whimpering sound, but she doesn't meet my eyes.

"Didn't you?"

Her throat bobs for a moment. "Yes," she whispers at last. "I just…wanted to be ready." Each word falls off her tongue with unquenchable shame and an equal amount of arousal. "Lara told me I'd get really horny, but I never realized…"

I let out a throaty chuckle. From here I can see her smooth bare ass. Her lower lips and upper thighs, shiny with slick. God, what I wouldn't do to drive into her right now. "Your body betrays you," I say with a grin. "You feel what you're doing to me?"

I lift my hips ever so slightly, just so she can feel the hard ridge of my cock pressing up against her. Janie gasps and it turns into a whine. "Yes," she breathes.

"I need to tell you something, and I need you to listen." I massage her ass, rubbing circles on the reddened flesh.

She nods.

"You will never question my authority as alpha again. Do you understand me?"

A few panted breaths, but finally, she hangs her head and relents. "Yes."

"Now I'm going to spank you five times. I want you to count each spank, and tell me who you belong to."

Another whimper escapes — music to my ears. Janie groans. Shifts in my lap. "Fine. But I have a request as well."

I almost burst out laughing at that. "You really think you're in any situation to be making requests? I'm not a pushover like Soren is with Lara. You should know that by now."

"And you should know that we both signed that contract, and if the ISA finds out that you're mistreating me…" Even in this disheveled state, the threat in her voice is clear.

Damn her.

"What's your request?" I say through gritted teeth.

She cranes her head just enough to make eye contact at last. "That we'll stop playing these games and I'll finally get to find out if you live up to all those big words." Janie places special emphasis on the word 'big' and my cock just about explodes right then and there. I can't believe it.

Someone so small, so beautiful…and yet so feisty.

I signed the contract expecting an emotionless exchange. A mere business transaction. But every time she challenges me like that, it makes me want to keep her to myself even more.

At this rate, I'm in for a long, *hard* year.

"You asked for it," I growl. I land my first spank on her left cheek and her whole body jolts with the movement.

"One!" She gasps.

"And who do you belong to?" I arc my hips upward to give her a little extra motivation.

"You!"

"Good girl."

So it goes — spanks interspersed with soft touches, everything to keep her guessing, to keep her wanting more.

By the time I reach five, we're both panting.

My cock can't wait any longer. With one last spank, I move my hand downward, landing the slap over her pussy lips instead. My fingers graze her swollen clit and she comes apart in my arms. Her soft body twitches like she's been struck by lightning. Tears roll down her face. Sweat and slick smears across her skin.

And we've only just begun. I'm barely able to hold back from what inevitably comes next.

FIRST MATING

JANIE

I've never came so hard in my life. What even *was* that? Rathgar brought me to the edge with such a mixture of pleasure and pain I nearly blacked out from the intensity of it all. He rights me carefully and lays me down on the bed. I let him move me the way he wants — my muscles are practically jello at this point.

I still feel aftershocks clench my core. Little throbs and twitches that do little to ease the burning ache within. I thought maybe once I came, I wouldn't feel so insane with lust anymore.

I was wrong.

If anything, I'm even more horny now, and the night's only just begun. Something tells me I'm not going to be getting much sleep tonight.

Between the omega heat and the earth-shattering orgasm I just had, my mind's in a fuzzy haze. Rathgar looms over me, all hard muscle and pure testosterone. Men like him get on my last nerve.

Until they make me come so hard I see stars, apparently.

Rathgar wastes no time after making sure I'm comfortable. He puts a pillow under my hips and lifts my legs up, eyes flashing with lust as he takes in the sight of my wet heat. I should cover myself. I should go and not let this brute of a man have his way with me.

But I signed a contract… Rathgar goes to his knees and buries his face between my legs, and I forget everything.

His tongue has gotta be longer than a human's. There's no way any man from Earth could eat me out the way he does. Or maybe I haven't been seeing the right men. Jack was my one and only before now, and he thought going down on a woman was 'gross'.

Rathgar had no such inclinations, if the way he feasted on my cunt was any indication.

"Fuck," Rathgar groans against me, large hands holding my legs on either side of his broad shoulders. "You taste…" He delves deeper with his tongue, mashing his face so close to me that his nose brushes my clit. "So fucking good."

I'm still coming down from my last orgasm, and Rathgar shows no signs of stopping. I try to squirm away, to give my body a chance to process all of these new sensations, but he's having none of it.

The more I try to pull away, the more he manhandles me. The more I struggle, the more ferocious his passion.

It's the sexiest game I've ever played — both of us testing each other, enjoying the push and pull of each movement and each sigh. This is so much better than that miserable excuse for sex that I had with Iris's father.

That was nothing. *This* is how you please a woman. I throw back my head into the fluffy pillows. My eyes, still unfocused and hazy, stare up at the intricate chandelier and the skylight above it. I'm trying to find some anchor to reality. Something to focus on besides the overwhelm and overstimulation of his tongue inside me. It doesn't work.

With a cry, I come again, my back arching off the bed as I cry out his name. Rathgar gives a satisfied grumble, looking up from his work.

"I like when you say that," he says, face covered with my juices. "Say my name again."

I turn my head again, sticking out my bottom lip in a pout without meeting his glance. This time, it's because I know it will get a rise out of him, and I want to see just how far he'll go.

His hands tighten on my thighs. It's a punishing, bruising grip that leaves me no room to move. "I said," he says in a tone that's all venom. "Say my name." And just to prove a point, he moves one hand down to my exposed sex and smacks it, just like during the spanking.

"A-aaah!" I cry out. The friction, the pressure, and the mix of pain with pleasure all drive me further to the edge, taking me to heights I didn't even know existed. How could he do all of this? And what's more, when did my body become so sensitive to his every touch?

"That's not my name," Rathgar growls. He laps over my clit with his wide tongue once, twice. He swirls around the bud over and over until my thighs are shaking with exertion and need, but just when I'm on the brink of collapse, he pulls away, a triumphant smile on his face.

"You want to come, don't you?" He wipes his face with the back of his hand. "You know what you have to do."

This time it's my turn to growl. It's not as deep or menacing as his. It surprises even me when it rumbles out of my throat, coming from somewhere deep inside. It doesn't even sound like me. But it *is* me.

The new me.

"You are full of surprises," Rathgar admits. He leans forward to kiss the sides of my legs. To caress my sides. Run his hands up to my breasts. Anything and everything to tease me, to make me stay on that precipice. But he doesn't take me over. Not yet.

"You know what you have to do," he says again, grin widening. "Tell me who you belong to, and I'll give you what you need."

You know what? Fuck pride. Fuck stubbornness. If I don't have him inside me right *now*, I'm going to lose my mind.

"Fine!" I cry out, and I'm glad we're in the middle of nowhere with carefully soundproofed walls. "You want me to say it? I'll say it. I'll shout it, even! I'm yours! Yours to pleasure and protect! Yours, Rathgar, yours, yours, yours, just *please—*"

And just like that, all of the passion he's been holding back erupts to the surface. "That's my good girl. Are you ready?"

I feel something hot and hard against my thigh, and I realize while I was shouting he'd freed his dick and repositioned himself to loom over me. I can't see it from this angle, but it's hot, heavy, and *huge*.

How am I supposed to fit that inside of me? And why does the challenge turn me on even more?

"I'm ready," I say through gritted teeth and closed eyes. As ready as I'll ever be.

The hot, bulbous head presses into my center, parting my lips only slightly at first. He's only begun, and already I suck in a breath at the stretch. My body tenses despite myself, and Rathgar's there to soothe me, to run careful caresses down my arms and side.

"Relax," he says in a more gentle tone than I've heard all evening. "Your body was made for this. All you need to do is relax."

I let out a slow, shaky breath. Relax. Right. But how am I supposed to relax when the biggest cock I've ever seen is trying to split me in two?

"Look at me." The words weren't harsh and commanding like they were before, but his power washed over me all the same.

My eyelids flutter open, and I'm greeted with the sight of him on top of me. He's so big, he blocks out most of the light, leaving a stark silhouette in his place. I should be terrified. Or disgusted, at the very least.

This was the last man I could ever see myself sleeping with, and yet? Here I was, pinned to the bed and at his mercy.

I swore when Jack left that I'd never let another man control me. But this? This is different. It doesn't feel so much like control as it feels like…a need. An empty space deep inside me, one I didn't even know I had. And with every touch, every word, he fills up those empty spaces.

Makes me feel whole again. Makes me want him even more.

It's almost certainly the hormones talking, but I consider the alternative. If I was going to do this, I might as well enjoy it, right? I can't imagine going through this with someone violent and cruel. Someone who cared little for my feelings or safety, only about getting his rocks off and getting out.

But Rathgar, for all his gruff exterior, shows that he knows more than just how to crack skulls. His rough, thick fingers get me off with such impossible precision. His tongue and teeth lap, nip, and kiss at all the right places, our bodies so in tune with one another it's like he's reading my mind.

God, I hope not.

I look up into his eyes, and the world stops spinning. He rests one calloused hand on the side of my face. The other braces on my hip. "Relax," he says again, and this time my body obeys.

Not only do I go slack under him, but my fears and worries melt away too. With a grunt, he pushes deeper inside of me. It's a stretch, but not an unpleasant one. The burn quickly turns into a throbbing pleasure center, feeling every ridge of his alien dick scraping against my inner walls.

My fingers dig into his flesh, my eyes wild and unfocused. He bends down to capture my lips in a hungry kiss before whispering in my ear. "Aaah, Janie — you're so fucking tight around me."

The dirty words make me clench my thighs around him. I get yet another growl as a reward. "Janie," he says again in that gruff tone, and I don't know if I'll ever get tired of hearing my name on his lips.

When he used it to deride me or tell me all the ways I was wrong, I hated the sound of his voice. Tried to avoid it at all costs.

But here in bed with him, it takes on a whole new meaning. He speaks it so reverently, like I'm the most precious treasure in the world.

I know better than to run with those thoughts. Silly fantasies like that were what got me into this mess in the first place. But damn, if he doesn't feel so *right...*

"Are you with me?" Rathgar asks. I glance up at him, realizing my thoughts had been elsewhere. "Are you hurt?"

"No." I let out a soft moan when I feel him sink all the way to the hilt. From this angle, he's pressing against my clit and I angle my hips upward in response. "It feels...good."

"Good," Rathgar says, gripping my hips with both hands. "Cause it's about to feel even better."

He hooks his arms under my legs, pulling them upward to thrust even deeper. The head of his cock nudges against my cervix and I cry out , arching against him.

That's all it takes for him to lose it completely — a feral growl rips free and he pulls out only to slam back in again. And again. And again.

He's pushing and pulling my hips in a bruising grip, grunting and panting like some kind of animal, and if I'm being honest? It's hot as fuck.

Guys, in my limited experience, didn't like to be vocal about their pleasure. I never knew if they were enjoying it or not. With Rathgar I had no such questions. He went at it like a man possessed — pumping into my body again and again with a wild look in his eyes and a snarl on his lips.

"Yes, yes, yes!" He groans when he angles upward, hitting the sensitive spot I like most. "Fuck, you feel so good, so tight…"

It doesn't take long before I'm grunting and panting along with him, slamming my hips upward with every thrust. He pushes, I pull. I wrap my legs around his back and hook my ankles. He's not getting away, and I don't want him to. We pant and groan and growl like beasts. When he shouts my name and buries himself in me balls deep, the hot splash of his cum against my tired walls sends me over the edge one more time, grasping and clenching and howling like the animals we are.

Alpha and omega, together as one.

My mind hazy, my limbs exhausted, I curl into his embrace. Darkness gathers and I can no longer fight it. The only hazy thought that floats through my mind before I drift asleep completely?

Good thing it's just Rathgar here with me. We're both just doing our job. Nothing more. Nothing less.

There's no chance I'd fall for a guy like him.

Right?

ANOTHER PROMISE

RATHGAR

Humans sure do sleep in curious positions. After she fell asleep in my arms, part of me wanted to lay there and fall asleep with her, too.

But another part of me, a bigger part now that the primal need to mate had died down, had something else on his mind.

I slip out from beneath her and crawl up into the rafters, lifting up the glass panel of the skylight and pulling myself up onto the roof.

First rule of field work — always secure the area before engaging. I'd already broken that one when I barged into the cottage and took her straight to bed. Any number of our enemies could be out here, laying in wait till I was most vulnerable.

I couldn't let that happen.

My whole life, my whole career hinged on constantly watching for danger. For anticipating it and neutralizing it before the enemy had a chance to act. It was that unfailing vigilance that earned me a spot at Soren's side.

I wasn't going to go soft now just because of a woman. A human woman, at that. What Soren does on his own time is his business, and I'm happy for him, but if he thinks I'm going to fall head over heels for an Earth girl, he's dead wrong.

Tell that to my still-racing heart.

I run a hand through my hair and turn to face the gentle night breeze. I focus on the surroundings and look for any weak spots, any vulnerabilities, but it's only a half focus.

My brain feels like a battlefield, and my heart? Even more so.

I still remember the way she cried out my name and clung to me like I was her lifeline. My muscles ache and my cock still remembers the soft heat of her insides. The way she tensed and throbbed around me, milking every drop of cum I had into her waiting womb…

"Fuck," I mutter. I screw my eyes shut and shake my head. This can't be happening. I have a job to do. My people — and my planet — depend on me.

I reacted the way any alpha would have in the presence of an omega in heat. It was simply a biological imperative. No feelings were part of it. She felt the same. She told me as much. And for that, I was at least, grateful.

Going into this with mismatched expectations would spell disaster for the both of us. We knew what we were getting into and we knew not to take it seriously. That would be that.

Or so I thought.

While I scan the perimeter, my brain drifts back to the time I saw her at the birthday party. The time when her little one so boldly ran up and clung to my leg.

A smile creeps across my face. Not so unlike her mother, that one. They both had a reckless streak a mile wide. And when Janie challenged me like she had in bed? It made me harder than I've ever been in my life. Like somehow, I was waiting all this time to find someone who could give as well as she got.

Too bad it's just a contract. Nothing more.

After I finish surveying the grounds, I slip back into the bedroom to find

Janie still sleeping soundly. My eyes linger on her for a bit longer than necessary — watching the way her body curls into the pillow, the way her dark hair splays out behind her on the mattress. My cock throbs at the sight of her still-naked breasts and her full, slightly parted lips.

Incredible...

Even though I've been trained in stealth, it's hard for a big guy like me to move without making some sort of noise. My footfalls must have woken her, because her eyelids flutter open, disoriented for half a second before she turns her head and sees me.

Her reaction is instantaneous. She lets out a low, pitiful whimper and draws her legs up toward her chest, pulling the covers ever closer. She looks…scared?

But why?

Had I done something wrong?

I take a step toward her, but she tenses even more. Only moments ago, we were tangled in ecstasy. Was she having second thoughts? Did I really scare her that much?

"Janie?" I ask softly, carefully. I extend what I hope looks like a peaceful hand. "Are you all right?"

She doesn't meet my gaze, opting to stare at the bed and chew her lip.

"What's wrong?" I try again.

Still nothing.

Now, I'm getting frustrated. Where was the fiery, feisty woman I took to my bed? Where was the needy omega who sang for me so beautifully as we drove each other to climax? She didn't really think I was going to *hurt* her, did she?

The thought disgusts me so much I wrinkle my nose and clench my jaw. My fist tightens before I realize I probably look like I'm angry at her. Not helping my case.

Still, I need to know where I stand. And I've never been one to tiptoe around a subject.

"Are you scared of me?" There, I said it. "Or do you think that since you're my omega, you're supposed to be sweet and submissive and weak in my presence?"

The words come out with more bite than I intend, but I can't stop the flood of emotion. The thought that someone would take advantage of her this way…it fills my soul with a deep, possessive anger. She doesn't deserve that.

Whether we're heart-mates or just two people doing a job, she's a woman and deserves to be treated with respect. Fertile females on my own planet are treasured above all else, treated like queens by their mates. I've seen the way Soren dotes on Lara and Iris. He's firm, but he is fair where it counts. That's our way. That's how we were raised, the code we live and die by.

Janie snaps her head up at my words, her eyes surprised and a little angry. "You're the big, bad alpha, remember? What were you doing, just hovering over my bed watching me sleep? Or were you about to run off too, now that you've finished with me?" Her voice cracks and her arms wrap around her knees.

My heart breaks for her. And more than ever, I want to tear that bastard that hurt her limb from limb. "I was simply checking on you," I snap back. "I wanted to make sure you were safe."

Janie snorts. "I've heard that one before. Every time I let a man into my life or my bed, I end up getting hurt."

I can't take it anymore. I lunge forward, letting the anger and emotion transform into something else. I cover her body with my own, my hands pinning her to the bed as I force her to look at me. Her breathing picks up and her skin heats under my touch, but she's not lost to the heat just yet.

She needs to hear what I have to say, and she needs to understand.

"Listen to me, Janie."

She gulps. Lets out a shuddering breath. Nods.

"I know you haven't had the best luck with men. I know there have been people that hurt you. If I could make it all go away, if I could avenge your pain and make it better…I would." I dip my head lower, next to her ear. She shivers at my touch, but doesn't pull away.

"Don't you understand yet? You're not on Earth anymore. I'm not one of them. Yes, we do things differently around here. That's not going to change. But you know what will change? The way you expect to be treated. Hear me now, and listen well: no Aesir man will ever harm you. It's the lowest, most dishonorable form of cruelty and cowardice. If I ever cross paths with that lowlife, you better believe he will regret the day he chose to abandon you."

Janie softens under my touch, her eyes wide. The tension's still there, but slowly, it's fading. Good. That means I'm getting through to her. I press a kiss to the pulse of her neck. Her ear. Her cheekbones. Her nose.

"While you are here, I, nor any of my men, will ever lay a hand on you without your consent. I would never, ever hurt a female I was not in combat with. Especially not…" I groan as her scent starts to swell again. "…my omega."

Janie slithers her hands up to cup the sides of my face, and I cover her soft palms with my own. I plant a kiss on her knuckles, then drop my head to capture her lips in a kiss.

I wish I could express myself better. I wish that I could tell her just how special she is and have her actually believe it. But this is all we have, for now, so I nuzzle against her and take in the sounds of her quickening breaths. The staccato beats of her heart.

And as her heat heightens, so too does my hunger. I use that to my advantage — to tease out those sensations and help her forget the past. I can't undo the way she was treated and I can't change what's already happened. But maybe, just maybe, I can give her enough good memories to replace the bad ones. And who knows. Maybe one day she'll look in the mirror and be proud of what she sees there.

As Janie softens beneath me and my cock jumps to attention, I draw out the moment, leaving her gasping and writhing before my dick's even out. It won't come close to expressing what I really feel...but it's enough.

CALL

JANIE

I sigh with relief and contentment as I ease into the steaming bath. After experiencing the best in Aesir luxury, I can see what Lara didn't want to leave. The bath-tub's more like a small spa, featuring more jets, nozzles, and scented soaps and lotions than I've ever seen in my life.

And to think that these people live like this…

It's a far cry from our old life, that's for sure. I lean my head back onto the pile of towels and stretch my legs, letting the hot water ease away my aches. My heat's finally going away, and although I can't deny it was fun, my body's ready for a little rest and relaxation.

Ever since my heat hit, the days seemed to blur together. If I wasn't having sex with Rathgar, I was thinking about having sex with Rathgar. It's terrifying, having something so all-consuming take hold of you on a daily basis. But also, kind of liberating?

I close my eyes and let the soothing massage of the water jets take me away. My mind drifts…and I find myself once again thinking of Rathgar.

Odd. I'm not even in heat anymore. Anyone would be hot for the nearest dick if they were all hopped up on hormones, but now? I had no reason to still be thinking about him. Right?

Even the tub feels a bit more empty without him in it. The last few times, I've bathed while wrapped in Rathgar's arms. I sit between his legs while he scrubs my skin and shampoos my hair. All the while he whispers such sweet nothings to me, words that would have fooled a younger me.

But I'm older and wiser now. I know it's nothing more than a chemical reaction for the both of us. I can appreciate the experience, remember it fondly, and move on with my life. That's that.

I wonder if he'll stick around once I go in for my physical and get the final test results. My stomach cramps at the thought. I remember all too well that fateful night when I confronted Jack.

He'd promised so much. Acted like he truly cared for me, like he would be there for me no matter what. In a matter of moments, all that changed with two pink lines on a plastic stick. I never heard from him again after that night.

Good riddance.

I think back to how passionate Rathgar got when I told him about it. How utterly shocked and disgusted he was that someone would do that. I scoffed. Maybe things really are different here, but it's all too common down on Earth.

Will Rathgar keep his word, or will he be yet another man that disappeared at the first sign of commitment?

Only time will tell.

After a long soak and plenty of time to think things over, I crawl out of the bath and wrap myself in one of the fluffy robes. The soft, plush fabric never fails to make me feel like a princess. After wrapping my hair in another towel, I step out of the bathroom and back into the main living area.

I half expect Rathgar to be there, waiting for me, but he's…not.

"Hello?" I call out. No answer.

I peek around corners and into every room. He's not there.

No matter. It's not like he has to stay here 24/7. He's Soren's second-in-command, after all. He probably just had some business to attend to.

It's actually kind of nice to have a day to myself, now that I think about it. Rathgar was an incredible and attentive lover, knowing my body almost better than I knew it myself, but we still had a ways to go in the socializing department.

Though he's softened up from his grumpy attitude pre-contract, he still has a surly disposition on the best of days. He grumbles about this and that, always finding something to worry about.

I shake my head. It's probably for the best that we aren't going to be together forever. He and I are just too different. So what if the sex is great? I've already been burned by a relationship like that before. That's why no one — especially not him — is going to break my heart ever again.

Sinking down onto the couch in the living room, I pull out my phone and scroll to Lara's number. It's different here on Aesir, of course. We had to get all new tech to match the networks here, but overall, the experience is mostly the same. Thank goodness for that.

Within a few rings, Lara picks up and I smile when I hear her familiar voice.

"Hey, Janie. You doing okay?"

"Yeah," I say, throwing my legs over the arm of the couch and laying backward. "I'm fine. Just had some downtime and thought I'd give you a call." I pause, then: "I miss you."

"I miss you too, sis. How are you holding up? The heat passed yet?"

I smile. "Do you really think I'd be talking to you if it hadn't?"

Lara chuckles. "True. I remember my first heat."

"You should have warned me!" I laugh along with her. Already, stress seems to flow away. No matter what happens with Rathgar, I still have her. That's what matters.

"How's Iris?" I ask when we're done gossiping. She's next on my mind, of course. There's more than a little twinge of guilt. Ever since she was born, Iris was the number one priority in my life. I promised myself that I would be the best mother I could and that I would never abandon her the way her father had.

This is the longest we've been apart since she was born, and I'm missing her something fierce. Now that the heat's gone and some semblance of rationality has returned, I can't wait to see my baby's face again. I need to hear her laugh. To hold her in my arms.

Even if I never have another child and this whole contract thing falls though, I still have her. She's my world, and no man — alien or otherwise — will come between us.

"Iris is fine. She's been a handful, but when isn't she?" Lara laughs. There's a sound of movement and then I hear a man's voice on the line.

"Hey, Janie. Good to hear from you. Lara's gone to fetch Iris so you can talk with her. How's everything at the cottages? Anything you need?"

"No," I answer honestly. "You guys really have everything here, huh?"

He lets out a low chuckle. "We pride ourselves on providing only the best for our females." A pause. "Rathgar isn't giving you a hard time, is he? I heard you two were matched together."

There's that lump in my throat again. That nagging, tugging feeling in my chest. It can't be that I actually have feelings for him. We'd just spent a lot of time together lately. And we'd had a *lot* of sex. It was normal for me to feel a little bit lonely now that he wasn't here.

"He's..." I start, but then Soren cuts me off.

"Here's Lara. Take care out there, all right?"

"Right..." I mutter, trailing off.

"Mommy?" Iris's soft little voice almost makes me forget about my conflicted heart. Almost.

* * *

THAT NIGHT, I lay in bed staring up at the stars through the skylight. It's the same as every other night since I came here, except for one thing.

I'm alone.

I roll over in bed, still smelling Rathgar's scent all over the pillows. Rationally, I know he's fine. I know he'll be back soon.

But as I drift into a troubled, fitful sleep, I can't help but worry that history's repeating itself all over again.

BREAKING TRADITION

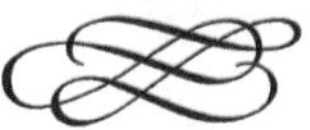

JANIE

I don't know why I thought things would be different when I woke up.

The moment I wake, I roll over and throw my arm over the side of the bed like I have every other morning. But there's something missing.

Or rather, someone.

I try not to think about it as I get out of bed and wash up in the bathroom. I focus on cooking breakfast in the kitchen, even though I'm subconsciously picking out Rathgar's favorite foods.

And I definitely don't think of him when I get dressed for the day and see one of his jackets there, hanging on the peg where he left it.

Sinking down onto the couch, I throw my head back and groan. I should be pleased. I should be relieved. I should be a lot of things, but all I feel right now is loneliness. Like something's missing, an empty space I never even noticed before.

Still grumbling to myself, I check the timeline on the paperwork from the

ISA. Now that my heat's over, they'll be sending nurses over to do checkups and pregnancy tests. Even at the thought of a test, my stomach cramps. I lay a hand over it gently and think about the possibilities.

Given how much Rathgar and I went at it over the last two weeks, it would be a shock if I *wasn't* pregnant. But then again, I hadn't had any symptoms or morning sickness, so…

I while away the morning picking through the selection of books tucked away in the living room. I still can't read the language very well, but there's one that looks like an atlas with plenty of pictures. No matter how long I stay on this foreign planet, it never fails to fill me with surprise and awe.

It's so beautiful and colorful, like something out of a storybook dream rather than a real, living breathing planet. But as I flip the pages, I see other regions of the world as well. Places far off that are less tropical and more rugged. It makes sense — a planet as large as Aesir's bound to have their own seasons and environments just the same as Earth, if not even more pronounced.

I wonder if I'll ever get to see one of the other regions. The mountainous one looks so pretty, all tall peaks and snow-capped ridges. I've never seen snow on a mountain before in real life.

I wonder if Iris would like to go sledding…

And there's that thought again. Iris. Family. Home.

I miss seeing my daughter. I miss being able to spend time with Lara and Ray. And even Soren.

If Rathgar's going to be gone for much longer, should I stay here and keep waiting? Or would I be better off with the comforts of home?

I pace around the living room for nearly half an hour weighing the options back and forth, but finally, I can't take it anymore. Orvox, the liaison for the ISA, told us to call if there was anything we needed or anything they could do to help. I figured it was just for emergencies, but staying here by myself was already starting to make me go stir crazy.

So with a deep breath, I pick up the phone and call Orvox over at the ISA.

It takes some convincing, but since my situation is unique, Orvox finally relents and grants me permission to return home. I tried to ask her if she knew where Rathgar had gone. She didn't answer. Either she really doesn't know, or she's not telling me. She doesn't hesitate to remind me that I'll still be subject to the terms of the contract and that I'll still need to be present for all the necessary appointments and tests, though.

I assure her that's not a problem. I don't plan on running off. I just want to go home. I gather up all my things, take one last look at the few belongings Rathgar left behind, and wait for the transport to arrive.

Looks like it's just me and my sis all over again.

It's funny how quickly I've come to call my house here in Soren's village home. Neither of us have been here very long, but the aliens have been nothing but hospitable and welcoming.

Of course, there's the fact that my sister is their leader's heart-mate. That helps. And I, as part of the family, get much the same treatment. It's nice — a far cry from our desperate living conditions on Earth. I don't know if I could go back to the way things were before.

I like not having to worry about where our next meal is going to come from. I like having space for Iris to play and learn and grow up. And I'm so proud to see that Lara's found a man who cherishes her more than life itself.

Everything seems so picture-perfect with them, and I'm happy for her, of course I am, but I can't help but want that for myself. Just a little.

My thoughts drift as I ride the shuttle back to the village. The cottages were nice, cozy places to stay, but they could never beat being home with my family and friends. It's almost dusk when we arrive back at Soren and Lara's house.

I raise my hand to knock on the door and it opens before I can do so, a beaming Lara standing there to greet me.

What a sight for sore eyes. I fall into her embrace and she welcomes me home. She doesn't ask what's going on with Rathgar, and for that I'm grateful. I was afraid she, or more likely Soren, would judge me for returning so soon. Would treat it as a rejection of my duties.

As if on cue, my stomach cramps again and my head spins. These cramps are coming on more frequently, but I tell myself it's just hunger. I was so stressed today I don't think I've eaten.

"Why don't we get you inside," Lara says, letting me lean on her. "There's someone who's very excited to see you."

The moment I'm in the door, there she is. Iris rounds the corner, toddling as fast as her little legs will take her. "Mommy!" She cries, holding her hands out to greet me.

All pain, all soreness or uncertainty, melts away the moment I see her face. She's what I do all this for. I pick her up, letting her small arms wrap around my neck. I've only been gone for a little over two weeks, and yet how does it seem like she's grown even in that time? I boost her on my hip and give her a kiss on the forehead.

"Hey there, baby girl. Did you miss me?"

"Miss…mama!" And she buries her face in my chest.

While I have her in my arms, things don't seem so bad. For a moment, I can almost pretend that I'm not almost-certainly knocked up by a grumpy alien warrior. I can pretend that things are normal. That life is normal.

Tears come to my eyes at last, and I sniff them away for a few seconds before letting them fall. It's just the hormones, I tell myself. It's just that I'm happy to be home with my family again. Not that I'm worried about Rathgar or the pregnancy or anything like that.

Certainly not.

"Janie!" Soren steps into the room after hearing our voices. "Didn't expect to see you here so soon. Is everything all right?"

"I…yes, I think so." The reality? I had no idea. Rathgar had up and vanished without a trace, and no one was telling me anything. Orvox forgot about one thing during our call, however. Rathgar's commander just so happens to be my brother-in-law.

If anyone knows where he's gone, it's him.

"Good," Soren continues. "I received a message from Rathgar earlier, by the way."

My eyes widen; my stomach cramps again. Here it was. The moment of truth. "Is he…all right?"

"It's my fault, really." Soren runs a hand through his hair and shakes his head. "I tried to talk him out of it, if you can believe me."

This didn't sound good. I sit down heavily on the couch and hold Iris close, waiting for the news. Any minute now, Soren's going to tell me that something's happened to Rathgar. That he's hurt. That he's not coming back.

That — heaven forbid — he's been killed.

"He didn't want you to worry, first and foremost." Soren points out. "He's alive and well, but he is leading a raid to a nearby tribe. Tensions have been…" he frowns, "shall we say, strained lately.

And they're showing their hand, meaning that we needed to make a move. I was going to go, but he told me it was important to him. Something personal, he said." He sighed. "He's a formidable warrior. One of the best. But to think he'd leave his omega alone in a time like this…" He shakes his head. "That man has more muscles than sense sometimes."

I can't help but chuckle, because while funny, it's also true. Rathgar is a lot of things, but calm and methodical isn't one of them. He takes action first and cleans up the fallout later.

In life, work, and in bed, I think to myself.

My mind aches with the realization. Of course, I knew that as Aesirheim's most prized warriors, they would be called to duty if the need arose. I guess I just…assumed that was all in the past.

Silly me. Peace and freedom always come at a cost.

"Do you know when he'll be back?" That's the first question on my mind, but it's far from the last. It's also the most innocent one I can think of right now.

"I don't know at the moment, but he's to keep me informed. I'll let you know if anything changes." He says it so easily, so casually, as if it were no more than a statement of fact. Maybe for him it is nothing more than a mission briefing, but for me, it's different.

Because it's not just my mind aching with this new revelation. My heart worries for him as well.

I tell myself it's just normal human compassion. I tell myself all kinds of things, but it's getting ever harder to believe them.

I can't be falling for Rathgar. I can't. It would ruin everything Lara and I have worked for and sacrificed so much for.

"There's one more thing." Soren catches my attention and pulls me away from my troubled thoughts. "He's offered up his home in the meantime. He asks that you stay there until he returns and that his personal house servants will prepare anything you desire."

"What? No!" The words tumble out before I can stop them. "I left the cottages because I couldn't stand being cooped up, waiting for him to return."

Soren's face is like a block of stone, cold and unreadable. "It is tradition."

I wrinkle my nose. "And what happens if I don't?"

Soren stays silent. "I don't know."

Holding Iris close and looking to my sister for support, I put my foot down. "I'm not going to be his caged bird. I'm staying here."

While Lara gives me an encouraging nod, Soren looks like I just told him the world was flat. At long last, he draws his mouth into a thin line and bows his head.

"Very well." I can hear how unhappy he is in the tone of his voice. Good thing Lara has him wrapped around her little finger as her heart-mate.

CELL

RATHGAR

The door splinters into a million fragments under the force of my boot. All the tech in the world won't save you if it's offline.

Finally, we've managed to corner the rival lord Kovarx at his opulent headquarters. He thought he could hide behind all his money and power and *stuff*.

Turns out even the most loyal followers will turn tail once there's no longer anything in it for them.

We'd been tailing Kovarx for months. Years, even. At every chance, he slipped through our fingers, using his virtually bottomless pocketbook to buy his way out of trouble. I was tired of being too little too late.

And I was tired of seeing the people suffer in poverty and squalor while he practically bathed in gold.

Makes me sick.

But all that comes to an end today. Right here, right now. The pathetic excuse for a man cowers in a corner, unguarded and unarmed. He doesn't deserve this land. He doesn't deserve to live.

And he doesn't deserve a fast, merciful death either.

Still, we have our orders. In and out. Claiming the land in Soren's name, vowing to bring it back under our banner, back to peace and prosperity.

"What do you have to say for yourself?" I roar, advancing on the so-called 'chieftain'. "Is this what you call honor? Hiding in a corner while your fields burn and your people go hungry?"

He doesn't answer and he doesn't meet my gaze. His expression is a mixture of rage and fear. The face of a man who knows his time has run out.

"Well, is it?" I lunge forward and grab him by the shirt collar, lifting him up in the air. His pitiful little legs flail and his body twitches in my grasp, trying to get free. Choked sounds come from his windpipe as his hands claw desperately at his throat.

"You think you can hide behind all your money and power like some kind of shield. You think it's all right for your people — the very people you swore to *protect* — to suffer while you live in luxury. Does it help you sleep at night? Knowing that a child starved to pay for your silk sheets?"

"I...please!" Kovarx wrenches out through strangled breaths. "You don't have to—you don't have to do this! We can make a deal!"

"The time for deals is long over, Kovarx. You had your chances. Too many of them! You've been a scourge upon this planet and these people for too long." I bare my teeth, making sure he feels the full brunt of my anger. "And now it's time for you to pay the price."

I snarl, swinging him toward the open window. It's a long way down. He doesn't even deserve this, but the thought of him frantically grasping at empty air in the second before his body shatters on the ground…

I should do it. I want to do it.

But in that split second, I stop. I think of Janie, out of nowhere. Think of her, back home and alone. She probably doesn't even know where I've gone. Doesn't know why I left.

So much for being a better man.

"H-here, we can do this! I have something you'll like, yes! My wife and child — take them, take them! I know your kind. You only live to take your pleasure and pillage. That's all you people want. Have your fun with them and let me be — please."

Red-hot fury pounds so loudly in my ears I can barely hear straight. My muscles bulge, my heart quickens. If he thinks me a savage, then I'll be one. A loud, feral roar breaks free as I slam him into the wall and let go, watching as he crumples to the ground. He's dazed, but not out yet. Now the little worm's on his hands and knees, begging and pleading for his life.

"Take me to them. Now." The words sound foreign even to my own ears.

Something deep and primal rose up within me the moment he tried to bargain his wife and child for his safety. Not only because it's utterly despicable, dishonorable, and downright evil…

But because of Janie, and Iris, and the little one that could be in Janie's belly right now. There it is. The Alpha instinct to claim, protect, and devour anyone and anything that gets in their way.

Starting with this lowlife piece of trash.

Kovarx scrambles to his feet and stumbles out of the room and down the hallway. I motion to my squad to stand down and let us pass. He leads us to a bare, nondescript door at the end of the hallway. Fishing a key out of his pocket, he unlocks it and pushes the door open.

"You see!" He cries. "They're very pretty, will serve you well—"

But I'm not listening to him. I'm staring at the woman and children huddled together in the cell-like room. There's only one bed and no windows. A stark contrast to the rest of the palace. Just what had he put this poor woman through?

The woman's pretty, but it's covered up by years of trauma and mistreatment. There's a bruise just below her eye and her hair hangs in awkward tangles. Her child isn't much better, a young girl with the same ruddy face as her mother and the most terrified eyes I've ever seen.

I've been through a lot in the wars. Seen a lot of terrible things, fought a lot of terrible battles. Made some decisions that haunt me to this day. But there's only one thing that drives straight to my heart like a knife. That cuts past all of my tough exterior and really, *really* wounds me.

And that's to see a child in pain.

"Get out." The words break on my trembling voice. "The both of you, get out, right now. We're going."

The child starts crying and the mother tries her best to comfort her, but I can tell she's just as scared.

All the while, Kovarx stands there with a smug grin on his face like he just made the deal of the century.

And he calls us the savages.

“Go on, you heard ‘im!” Kovarx barks, and they flinch at the mere sound of his voice.

Gods.

Slowly, the trembling mother and her child near the door. I turn and motion for Mina, our medic, to come forward.

They cross the threshold, still wailing and quaking and trembling. They can hardly keep their balance, unsure steps and bare feet. They visibly tense when they walk past Kovarx.

Oh, he is going to *regret* this. And he'll have plenty of time to think about his choices…

As soon as the mother and child are out of range, I come down on him hard with the butt of my sword, bashing him in the back of the skull. He drops like a sack of potatoes and I grab the key that clatters to the floor.

Picking him up by the collar again, I toss him unceremoniously into the cell and slam the door. "Enjoy your stay, *my lord*." Every word drips with venom, with vengeance for all those he wronged. And especially for the mother and child.

With that, I shove the key into the door and snap it in half. He'll never see the outside of this cell again, and even that's much too merciful a punishment for someone such as him.

But in the moment, it's enough. Blood still boiling, I turn back to my squad and we prepare to leave the building. The mother and child are still crying, but in Mina's capable hands. I just hope they can learn to trust, to let us help. I know not what torture he put them through, but on my honor as a soldier and an Alpha, I will never let that happen to any woman or child ever again.

Thoughts of Janie flash through my mind once more, only steeling my resolve. My cock jumps at the thought of her sweet heat enveloping me once more. Battle always did get my blood up, and this time it was personal.

I know she's just my contract surrogate, but I need to see her. I need to make sure she's all right. Janie's back at the cottages without me, probably thinking I gave up on her too, as the lowlife who fathered Iris did.

I don't know how I'm going to make it up to her, but I vow right then and there that I'll do whatever it takes to see her smile and trust me again.

FIGHT OR FLIGHT

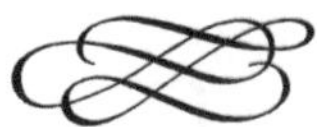

JANIE

THREE MONTHS AFTER RATHGAR VANISHED

It has been three months, and I haven't heard a peep from my so-called 'mate'. He's just another sperm donor at this point, running off when he gets cold feet.

I should have expected it, really. Should have known better than to trust a man again. But at least I have Iris, Lara, and Soren.

That will have to be enough.

The nurses come by almost every day lately, or at least it seems like it. I got a positive pregnancy test only days after Rathgar left. What should have been a happy occasion only shadowed with worry and uncertainty.

Another absent father.

Soren tries to comfort me. He tells me that Rathgar is away on a mission, that he would be here if he could, but their operation ran into some complications. Whatever that means.

I know Soren and Rathgar are best buddies, but Soren's no nonsense attitude wouldn't let him lie about Rathgar, even for my sake. Soren insists Rathgar will come back, but I'm tired of waiting.

When?

I've been staying with Lara and Soren all this time, and the nurses tell me I'm heading into the second trimester. *One down, two to go.* My belly is starting to swell and even Iris notices, tapping a hand on the baby bump when I hold her in my lap. I try to tell her she will have a new baby brother or sister on the way, but I don't think she understands. That's okay. She will soon enough.

I'm eating breakfast with Lara, Soren, and Ray when Soren's tablet pings and he looks up. "It's them."

My heart leaps into my throat. “Them…?” I start.

Soren nods. “I’ve just gotten word. Rathgar and the rest of the war band will be returning today.”

“Today?” I croak, nearly choking on my cereal. All this time I’ve been waiting, and now that it’s here I don’t know what to do. I’ve been holed up here, hiding from the future and hiding from my duty. I know Soren doesn’t approve of me staying here. He says that an omega female, especially one that’s with child, should stay in the domicile provided by her alpha male.

And that would make sense, you know, if he was actually here.

Soren gives another curt nod. He furrows his brow, scrolling through the announcement on his tablet. "Hmm." He says, and puts the device away.

I don't like the sound of that. "What's 'hmm'?" I try to play it off as mere curiosity, but the truth is I need to know if Rathgar's okay. If he even remembers me at all.

Soren levels his gaze at me. It's the cold stare of a hardened general, but I stand my ground. "Rathgar did ask about you."

My heart leaps and my stomach flips more times than the pancakes we ate this morning. "Oh?" I try to sound casual, but the waver in my voice betrays me.

"Yes." Soren says. He links his fingers together and rests his chin on them, observing me from across the table. I squirm, but I don't look away. "He wants to know how you're enjoying the lodgings he so kindly prepared for you."

Oh.

I didn't expect that. Guilt comes first, starting in my throat and working its way down to my chest and stomach. I knew it was tradition, but when he put it like that…

I closed my eyes and took a deep breath through my nose. No. I'd made this decision because it was best for me, Iris, and the baby. That's what mattered, not what Rathgar thought.

He hadn't even been here for three months!

Next came anger. My fists clenched under the table. He left without a word — after the best sex of my life, mind you — and expected me to stay alone in an unfamiliar house, just waiting for him?

Preposterous.

Lara silently gripped my hand from her seat beside me. "It's been a joy having you here, but now that he's back…"

I gulped. The time that I spent with him felt like heaven. I was just getting used to the fact that maybe, a man actually cared about me for once. That he wanted to make a real go of it, to care for a growing family.

Now I didn't know what to think.

A carnal part of me quivered in excitement and anticipation. It had been so long, and I couldn't wait to see him again. But would it be the same?

I bit my lip and let out another breath, shaking my head. "He can come get me if he wants me." I paused, debating the last words, and then: "I will not wait for a man."

Soren's eyes flash at the perceived insult, but what's he going to do? Lara's right there, as well as our children.

I stand up from the breakfast table, my mind still reeling. Thoughts fly back and forth across my brain, busier than the spaceport at rush hour. I wanted him. I hated him. I needed him. He left me. I wasn't going to bow to his wishes. But he'd been nothing but good to me, at least in the time we were together…

"I'm going for a walk." I say. "I need to clear my head."

"Mama?" Iris says, looking up at me with wide, innocent eyes. Her smile breaks through some of the pain and confusion.

"Want to go for a walk, Iris?" I crouch down so we're eye level. "We can go see the mushrooms at the lake. Would you like that?"

I guess I said the magic word, because she pushes herself out of her seat and starts toddling toward the door.

"All right, all right. I'm coming." With a hopeful wave at Soren and Lara, Iris takes my hand and we step out into the warm breezy day.

Soren's house connects to a nature trail, leading to a crystal-clear lake and some of the most amazing flora I've seen in my life. Iris's favorite part is the mushrooms. But these aren't just any mushrooms. Apparently on Aesirheim, they're more like trees. They grow that large, too!

Walking underneath their wide, colorful caps always makes me think about huddling under a hundred umbrellas. I take the opportunity to teach Iris about colors, pointing to each of the mushrooms in turn and repeating the color back to her.

We reach the lake and sit down on the soft moss, watching as the many-winged birds flock by above us. Iris has her shoes off, dipping her toes in the water. I'm staring out across the placid surface, trying to figure out what to do with my life.

The breeze changes direction and as it rustles through the mushroom forest, I catch a familiar scent. The sharp tang of copper mixed with a homier, cozier scent like a crackling fireplace. I know it's familiar, but from where?

That's when I hear footsteps. Large, heavy footsteps.

I pull Iris in, holding her close and listening. I don't know what I'm afraid of — this area is extremely safe, and no one would dare attack so close to Soren's home. But a raw, primal fear grips me and won't let go.

I feel like cornered prey. Like a deer in the headlights, too shocked to move. My breaths shudder out one by one as the steps grow closer. Even Iris must realize something's up, because she grows quiet for the first time in what seems like forever.

Fight or flight. The words echo in my mind, over and over. Why am I like this? I'm not in any danger. So why do I feel like a terrified rabbit, about to run for cover?

The smell intensifies, and when I hear his voice my reaction makes sense:

"So, this is where my omega's run off to."

RAHRAH

RATHGAR

The entire time I was away, Janie always stayed at the forefront of my mind. I hadn't planned to be gone for so long, especially when she was so early in her pregnancy, but what choice did I have?

I made a promise to Soren and to Aesirheim long ago. I pledged to always serve the planet and its people, no matter the consequences.

And I'd done that. At long last, we'd finally caught the man we'd been hunting for years. But at what cost?

I thought I would see her when I arrived home. I thought she would be there. That was part of the mating process. I made sure that she would have everything she needed when I was away. It was my duty as a man and as an alpha.

But she'd refused it all. She hadn't even visited the house I prepared for her. Not once.

Was she unhappy with our mating? Or did she distrust me that much?

Confusion, fear, and anger bubble up inside of me, alpha instincts pressing to the fore. Everything was as I'd left it. All clean and tidy and polished for her arrival. But she never arrived.

For a split second, panic squeezes at my heart. What if something had happened to her? To the baby?

But one step outside and one sniff tells me everything I need to know. She's here, all right. And close. So why has she rejected me like this?

Janie is from another world. I know that. She isn't expected to know all of our customs. But she has Lara and Soren, not to mention the ISA. Surely they would have briefed her.

My hands ball into fists and I growl, deep in my chest. Rejecting my offer is akin to rejecting my status as alpha. And I can't stand for that.

Reason flies out the window and rationality takes a backseat. I start stomping toward the source of her scent, ready to give her a piece of my mind. Why must she defy me at every turn? Why must she test my patience so?

And then I remember how the flush of her cheeks matched the flush of her *other* cheeks the last time I punished her. The combination of fear and arousal in her eyes. The way she got off on me manhandling her, talking dirty and taking what I wanted.

Was she planning this?

Now I can sniff her out like prey. I tear through the brush like a predator, heart leaping as my mate grows nearer and nearer. Her sweet, perfect scent shifts and changes the closer I get. It takes on more depth, a second, subtle note joining the first.

She's pregnant.

That thought pushes me to run faster. To reach her sooner. To scold her for being out here alone, for being so careless, for being so…

Wait. She's not alone.

"Rahrah!" The tiny voice breaks the silence and little arms pull away from her mother's. She starts running toward me again, just like the last time.

And just like the last time, I'm shocked speechless. In the child's dark eyes, I see hints of her mother. In the curve of her smile. The soft waves of her hair.

It's like a looking glass into the future. A premonition of what's to come. I knew it ever since signing the contract, but seeing that little girl toddling toward me makes me realize it for the first time:

I'm going to be a father.

The anger and disdain floods out of me in an instant, replaced with a warm, suffusing presence that surprises even me. I crouch down and let her run into my arms, picking the girl up and letting her wrap her arms around my neck.

She's light as a feather. So much different from young in our world. Her big, curious eyes light up and she squeals with excitement. In that moment, I've never felt so unprepared. So utterly disarmed.

Is this…what being a father feels like?

Janie laughs and walks toward us, her eyes soft and unreadable. Her gaze is only fixed on Iris, on the way she moves and grabs and laughs in my arms. She doesn't even look at me.

And to be honest? I probably deserve that.

I thought I was doing the right thing by giving her land and housing and all the luxury our planet had to offer. I thought she'd be grateful.

Looks like I still have a lot to learn about these Earth women.

"Soren's been telling Iris about you." Janie's first words to me are calm, measured. No hint of emotion or excitement either way. "He tried to teach her your name, but as you can see…" Her lips pull upwards, ever so slightly, but even that takes my breath away. "Iris hasn't quite got it yet."

"Rahrah," Iris repeats, this time weaving her fingers into my braid. I'm sweaty, tired, dirty, and probably caked with blood. Yet this little one, so innocent and pure, runs to me as if I were her own father. Calls out my name, garbled as it is. Wraps her arms around me like I'm the most precious thing in the world.

And something shifts in my heart, just then. This child — and this woman — need me. Not in a helpless way. In a way I thought I'd never feel for anyone, and certainly not an Earth woman:

Family.

"Let's go," I say, and this time I can't keep the emotion from my voice.

Janie doesn't argue. Doesn't resist. She fixes me with that same awestruck, doe-eyed stare, and I turn toward home, holding Iris in my arms. I resolve to fix everything.

NEST

JANIE

Well, this is it. I've put off the inevitable for as long as possible, but now that Rathgar's back, I'm finally walking with him toward his home.

Correction: *our* home.

I try to ignore the way my heart leaps in my chest as I see his strong arms encircling Iris. It's tender, almost. Completely different from his usual demeanor. And to think, he stomped over to where we were staying, furious…

The mean, surly warrior is utterly helpless in the face of a child. If I wasn't trying to keep things professional between us, it could have been adorable.

Something I could fall in love with.

He's already left me once. Who's to say he won't do it again? No matter what happens, I won't put my heart on the line again. I can't.

* * *

THE MOMENT I step into the house, I can already tell it's going to be different. Warm, soft colors and natural tones accent all the furniture and decorations, while huge windows let in the afternoon sunlight.

While Soren's house has a very modern look with lots of steel and bronze, Rathgar seems to have taken the opposite approach. It's very cozy, welcoming, and the plants and flowers scattered everywhere makes it feel like I'm still outside.

"What do you think?" Rathgar asks under his breath. He puts Iris down at last. Her first inspection is to plop down and run her fingers over the textured carpet.

"It's…" I look around and struggle for the words. "It's beautiful. You put all this together for me?"

Wow. I wasn't expecting to actually feel guilty. The man left me without a word! For months!

But when I look around at all the thought and care he put into the layout and decorations, I realize he was thinking about me all along. Little accents, like the time I told him my favorite flower was the lily, brighten up the space. He's customized everything all the way down to the direction the windows face because I hated getting woken up by the sun.

All those times I thought I was just talking to hear myself talk. He'd grunt and move on to something else, but he'd heard me. He listened and filed it all away for later.

For this.

My amazement grows with each room I visit. It has to be the pregnancy hormones, but seeing all this just makes me want to curl up with as many blankets and pillows as I can find. A little nest, just for me and my baby. That sounds nice.

Iris makes a beeline for the door at the back of the house and it's the one room I haven't visited yet. Rathgar follows behind me. When I crack open the door, I clap a hand to my mouth in shock.

A child's bedroom. A sweet, soft room filled with an Iris-sized bed, a collection of colorful toys, and what's more — a huge mural next to the bed, depicting the mushroom forest.

How…how did he know all this?

"Look!" Iris says with delight, running forward and pointing at the painting. "Red!"

I look over my shoulder at Rathgar. He shrugs so nonchalantly, as if this isn't the most amazing thing anyone's ever done for me in my whole life.

"How did you…why did you…" The words clutter on my tongue and won't come out.

"What?" He raises an eyebrow. "All this?"

"Yeah…" I gesture around at everything. "It's so…"

"Anyone would do the same. I know you're not…you know…staying, or anything. But I still like to follow the old ways." Rathgar rubs the back of his neck, avoiding my gaze.

He keeps talking, but those few words play on repeat in my brain.

Not staying.

Not staying.

He's right, of course. As nice as this place was and as much trouble as he must have gone through, it was only temporary. And it was going to take more than a few throw pillows to forgive his absence.

Forcing myself back on track, I realize I haven't seen my bedroom yet. There's Rathgar's, which has all the warmth and charm of a forest enclave, but…

"Um, Rathgar?"

"Hmm?"

"Which one is…I mean, where's my room?"

His face turns, as if I've just spoken gibberish. I tap at the translator over my ear. Nope. Still working. Rathgar closes the distance between us, putting a hand out to pin me against the wall.

He's so close like this. So large and intimidating and so deliciously *alpha*. His scent floods my system and my gaze softens, roaming over every muscled ridge of his body. My mouth goes dry, but wetness seeps between my thighs.

He smells it, too. I know he can by the strangled groan he makes in the back of his throat. If there's a sexier sound in the world, I don't know about it.

Something about having such power over this huge, intimidating warrior turns me on like nothing else.

Knowing that it's my body and my scent making him feel this way. Knowing that the growing bulge in his pants is for me and me alone.

"I thought you knew," he says gruffly. I shiver as his deep voice washes over me. There's nowhere to run, nowhere to hide. He's got me caged in against the wall by his strong arms and massive body.

Sparks of longing flare to life once more, taking seed in my belly and moving deeper down.

"You're going to be staying with me."

Oh. "You mean that room..."

"It's your nest now. This is our way. Come." He straightens and backs away from me, putting his arms down so I can move.

I let out a shuddering breath and my heart beats a couple extra times to catch up. Why does the space left between us suddenly feel so empty?

A *nest,* he'd called it. And as we walk into the bedroom together, some deep, omega part of me finds joy in that. A place of safety and comfort. A place to call my own.

I yawn and an almost untamable urge passes. Me, curled up in bed with Rathgar at my side. Me, belly round with child as we read a story to Iris together.

Me, with our new baby, showing them the wonders of this new world.

It's just like the dream I had as a child. To grow up and be a mother and a wife and build a good, happy life with the people I loved.

It couldn't be with Rathgar. It could never be with Rathgar. I'm worried that I'm setting myself up for heartbreak. But for the next few months that we could have together, would it be so bad to pretend?

MOST PRECIOUS GIFT

RATHGAR

Sometimes I wonder if I made the right choice. If I acted too rashly. But the thought of Janie staying with another alpha — even if it is Soren, a man I trust with my life — has me seeing red.

I thought these urges were supposed to pass after Janie's heat was over. We did what we signed up to do. She's pregnant, and well on her way to birthing a healthy Aesir child.

So why does her mere presence still drive my instincts crazy? There's nothing I'd love more than to throw her in bed and *show* her just how much I missed her, but there's not much I can do when she has a child in tow.

Make that two, if you count the one forming inside her.

I still haven't forgotten how she rejected my advances, nor have I forgotten that she chose to break with tradition and stay with her sister instead of the housing I prepared for her.

She's single-minded and stubborn, which is endearing in its own way, but if she does not learn her place in our society, she will continue to have trouble. And by extension, *we* will continue to have trouble.

Janie tests my patience in every way possible. As a mate, as an alpha, as a man, and as a father. I've put everything into making sure that she and Iris have everything they need for the pregnancy and beyond. It's simply my duty as an alpha. It's part of the contract we both signed. Nothing weird about it.

At least, that's what I keep telling myself.

But with each day that passes, I'm finding that harder and harder to believe.

"Iris, no!" My ears perk up at the sound of Janie's panicked yelp. Jumping to my feet, I run into the kitchen, ready to defend them if need be. But what awaits me is much less dangerous…and much more adorable.

Iris sits on the kitchen tile, mouth and hands smeared with dark red juices. She's somehow even gotten it on her clothes and on her bare feet. For a moment it almost looks like blood, and it's unnerving how worried that makes me. Plump, juicy berries, picked just this morning, are all over the floor and around her. On the counter is the overturned basket. She simply looks up at us with an innocent smile and raises her berry-stained hands to her mouth again.

Janie's already picking up the berries and trying to scoop them back into the basket, but I step in before she can get much further. "Allow me."

She gasps when she realizes I've been watching, and her hand covers her mouth as well. "Oh, I'm so sorry, Rathgar! I didn't mean to make a mess, I had my back turned for one moment and she tipped over the basket, I'll clean it up, I promise—"

"Hey." I take her wrist, applying enough pressure for her to look up at me, eyes wide and embarrassed. Why does she continue to cower before me like this? Am I that unapproachable? "It's all right."

Janie's mouth opens then closes again. Even though she's distressed, the sight of her soft, pouty lips so close to mine makes me want to claim her all over again. This time it's more than just a feral lust, though — something twinges at my chest, deep within. Something I've heard about only in legends and stories…

But it couldn't be. Not with her.

"You can wipe down the counter and I'll get Iris cleaned up." I don't leave room for her to question me. She needs to rest, not spend all day chasing after Iris. Janie acts like she's the only one that can care for her, but she forgets that I'm right here.

And, whether I want to admit it or not, I kind of like looking after the girl. "Come on, little one." I crouch down to her level and hold out my hand. She plops her much smaller hand in my own, along with a couple bruised berries.

"Are these for me?" I ask, smiling down at her. I can't help but smile when I'm around her. I tell myself that it's because children are so rare for our race, we've learned to treasure them above all else.

But this goes beyond duty. When she looks up at me with those soft, innocent eyes and calls out her nickname for me, my heart melts just a little more.

"Let's get you cleaned up." I take her into my arms and we go to the washroom together.

As I gently wash Iris from head to toe, my heart continues to pound and thump in my chest. A sharp zing like a shock races down my spine and travels to each of my fingers and toes. I'm utterly powerless and vulnerable before this little girl, and that's perhaps the most damning revelation of all.

I told myself I wouldn't get involved. Neither of us planned for forever.

But my heart, and my body, seem to have other ideas.

I need some time to clear my head. To understand these new and unfamiliar feelings. After making sure that Janie and Iris are settled, I excuse myself and head to the training ground, hoping that the physical activity will do me some good.

Because if I really am falling for her — if she's really my heart-mate? That changes everything.

* * *

"THOUGHT I'D FIND YOU HERE."

I'm halfway through a punishing set of drills when I hear Soren's footsteps approach. I don't even have to look behind me. I know it's him.

I let my weapon drop, shoulders sagging with exhaustion and breath coming out in ragged gasps. I don't turn to face him. Not yet.

"Something's bothering you." Again, it's not a question. Soren and I have fought together longer than any of the others. When you've worked together for so long, you pick up on things.

I press my lips together, not willing to admit it. With a cry I lunge at the target again, trying to let the pain and exertion cloud over everything else. Trying to lose myself to battle, just like I always did before.

Then Soren's hand falls on my shoulder. "Rathgar." His intonation changes instantly, no longer a friend, but a commander.

I turn to him at last, straightening my posture and giving him our salute. "Sir."

Soren's face remains stoic. Only his eyes give away the concern within. "What brings you all the way out here? Surely I thought you'd be spending time with your omega. You must have missed her very much."

I swallow. There's no getting around it, was there? I chew on the words for a moment, still unsure what to say. How can I articulate the utter storm of emotions and fears bubbling through me? How can anyone understand?

"Can I…ask you something?" I say at last.

Soren nods. "Speak freely."

Once those words cross my lips, I know there's no going back. But if anyone knows what I'm going through, it's Soren. "How did…" I furrow my brow and break eye contact, my face flushing. "How did you know? About Lara, I mean."

Soren tilts his head. His eyes tell me he already knows what I'm going to say, however. "What about her?"

Damn him, he wants to make me say it. Out loud. "How did you know that you were in love?"

Soren chuckles. A knowing smile spreads across his face. "Now that's quite the question. That's what's got you all tied up in knots?"

There was no use hiding it any longer. "Yeah."

"Come on." His voice was softer now. Kinder. "Let's get a drink. You look like you could use one."

"Yeah," I say at last. Some of the weight lifts off my shoulders just at the offering. I'm not exactly good at talking about my feelings, and to do so with my commanding officer? I didn't know what to expect.

But he was more than just my boss. He was my best friend, and my brother in all but blood. We looked out for one another, no matter what happened. And that included matters of the heart.

So I put down my weapon, cleaned up the mess I'd made, and followed Soren to the tavern, hoping to find some answers — or at least, some clarity.

"SHE'S A SPECIAL ONE, you know. Janie." Soren says over a full mug of dark Aesir ale. It sparks and fizzles on the tongue before going down smooth.

One of my favorites, and a staple when we were deployed.

"She is." Special. That was one way to put it. I could think of a million other words to describe what she did to me, but none of them could come close to the truth. "I just…never expected to get paired with her. Never expected to be part of this program at all. I was only doing this for you, remember?"

"I know." Soren smiles and takes another sip. He wipes his mouth with the back of his hand and observes me, chin resting on his hands. "Sure, I was a bit more enthusiastic about my prospects, but I still didn't expect to find my heart-mate." His eyes glaze over the way they always do when he talks about Lara. I used to find it uncomfortable, but in the wake of everything that's happened, it's kind of endearing.

"So when did I know?" Soren continues, tilting his head in thought. "It's not like I had a sudden revelation or anything. It's the little things. The way she smiled. The way her body felt against mine. The way I felt when I thought about losing her..." He sighs and shakes his head. "It's when I realized that I could not go back to the way things were before. That she had wormed her way into my heart and soul, and I couldn't see a life without her in it." When he smiles this time, his eyes are far away. Wistful. "I knew I'd do whatever it took to keep her safe."

"Janie's..." I don't know how to start. Much less, how to explain the jumbled mess of fears and confusion in my mind. "She's not like Lara. She's energetic and kind-hearted, but seems to take issue with the way I treat her. It's almost like she's scared of me, despite everything I've done to the contrary." I stare into my drink, looking for answers in the dark bubbles. "I don't know what I've done wrong. Maybe I'm just not cut out for this mating thing."

"I wouldn't jump to that conclusion just yet." Soren waves down the bartender and orders another round. I know I need to get back home and back to Janie, but Soren and I hardly ever get to talk anymore. And this is important.

"So what should I do?" I mutter, more to myself than to him. "Is she actually that scared of me? Did she say anything to you or Lara when she was staying there?" Maybe I was missing something. If Janie would talk to anyone about it, she'd talk to her sister. Maybe Soren had overheard something.

"I know you're a good listener, Rathgar. And I know you're a details man. Think. Did she talk about her past at all?"

I frown, thinking back. Little by little, her words came back to me. Her fears. Her troubles.

Not to mention how angry and how protective I'd gotten over her mistreatment. "Her ex. That's what this is about."

Soren nods. "I do believe so. It's not so much that she's scared of you.

She's been traumatized by men in general, and at such a young age. Think about it. Imagine losing your parents. Your job. Having to struggle to make ends meet and put food on the table, all while carrying a child."

When he put it like that…

My fists clench under the table and my heart squeezes with unbidden emotion. The slime ball that left her better be glad he's not in the same solar system, or he'd be getting a piece of my mind.

"And that's not all," Soren continues. "She's got to look after an infant on her own, with only her sister to count on for company. They were so desperate that Lara signed up for the ISA, remember? That's how they came here in the first place."

"Oh yeah…" My face falls. I'd spent so much time paying attention to the wrong details, when I didn't stop to think that this was all such a huge change for her. Add on to that her bad experiences with men, and no wonder she was still skittish.

"She is still new to our world, Rathgar. As is Lara, for that matter. It is not easy to adjust to an entirely new planet. A new culture. A new atmosphere. Surely you remember our early days patrolling the Fringe?"

"Boy, that takes me back." I finish my drink and lean back in my chair, reminiscing about the days gone by. Soren and I had explored the far reaches of the galaxy and had to spend months on inhospitable planets with nothing but our wits to guide us. We made it through, but those were tough times.

The difference was, we'd trained our entire lives for that kind of thing. Lara and Janie had not.

"In the face of everything they've gone through, I daresay Janie is one of the bravest women I've had the fortune to meet. Her and Lara both." His eyes mist over again, and my thoughts turn to the woman staying in my home.

My omega.

"All those months you were gone, Rathgar, she was terrified. She thought you'd given up on her just like every other man in her life had. I know you had your order, but you should have known better. Should have done better. But you still have a chance to make it right. Go to her. Her and Iris both. And think about this: when you were gone and she was still vulnerable and needy, she could have gone to any male, any alpha she wanted."

I tense and push myself up from the table, muscles reacting on instinct. Soren simply holds a hand up to stop me. "But she didn't." He makes sure I'm paying attention, and then, "because she was waiting on you."

Oh. *Oh*. I don't know what I expected, but it wasn't that. She acted like she'd rather be anywhere else most of the time. She defied me at every turn.

And now this?

"Give her time, Rathgar." Soren says before standing and taking the mugs back to the bar. "She's a strong woman, and a powerful omega. You two aren't that different, when you think about it."

As Soren walks with me back to our homes, I do think about it. By the time we part ways, I have a new plan to win Janie over. Not with brute force or lavish gifts, but with the most precious resource of all: time.

NESTING INSTINCT

JANIE

"That was fun, huh, Iris?" We're both carrying baskets stuffed full of mushrooms after a successful morning helping in the gardens. They're nothing like the towering mushroom forests that Iris loves so much, but they're hand-sized and perfect for cooking.

Iris swings her basket back and forth happily, humming a tune as we walk down the path back home.

As my pregnancy progresses, so too does my 'relationship' with Rathgar. I say that in quotes because I'm still not really sure what we are. Contract mates, yes. A surrogate for the alpha? Of course. But my feelings beyond that elude me even on the best of days, and he's not exactly forthcoming with his own.

I'm thinking about something Lara told me, about when she first fell for Soren. I remember our conversation well, even though it feels like forever ago now. Hearing her voice for the first time after months of being stuck on Earth was the greatest gift I could have gotten. Little did I know I would soon be joining her among the stars.

When my sister first told me that she had feelings for an alien, I didn't know what to think. I worried for her, most of all. Neither of us had the best track record with human men, so what would make alien men any different? But it wasn't only that. A shred of jealousy colored my thoughts back then. A fear that I'd lose my only sister to a man and never see her again.

An unfounded fear, luckily. But as I review the feelings we shared that day, I come to realize that while my relationship with Rathgar has been anything but smooth, I'm starting to feel something for him as well.

And really, it's hard not to when he's so good with Iris. Any man good with kids is a winner in my book. Especially after what happened with Iris's father. If I ever settle down with a man, he will have to accept all of me, my daughter Iris included. She's the center of my life, and any man in my life has to understand that she will always come first.

I thought it was a pipe dream. That it would take a miracle. But then Rathgar crashed into my life — almost literally — and challenged everything I thought I knew.

We reach the house at last and I take Iris's basket, handing her the key and teaching her how to unlock the door. When we push it open, I'm surprised to see Lara standing there. A brief moment of panic halts my steps, but as the door opens further Rathgar's standing there as well.

I let out a breath. For half a second, I feared Rathgar had disappeared again. That something had happened to him, and he wouldn't be coming back this time. And that scared me a lot more than it should.

"Rah-rah!" Iris calls out, waving at him with both hands and a cheesy grin.

Lara greets me with a warm hug and takes the baskets off my hands while we both go into the kitchen.

"What brings you out here?" I ask as casually as I can while we put away the day's haul.

A grin creeps at the corner's of Lara's face. She's never been good at hiding her emotions, and I see through her right away. "You're scheming again, aren't you?"

Lara barks out a laugh and presses a hand to her chest in mock affront. "I would never." The twinkle in her eyes says otherwise. "I simply came at Rathgar's request. I'm doing him a favor."

"Oh?" I ask while I duck into the pantry, moving the jars and preserves to make space for the mushrooms. "And what's that?"

"He says you two have plans tonight?" Her tone ends in a question. One that begs to know all the juicy details.

"Plans…" I mutter, my brain rushing to catch up. "Oh! I mean, we were planning to have dinner together, but I would hardly call that 'plans'. And Iris always joins us for dinner, why would he…"

Lara cuts me off. "Why would he, indeed." And with a wink she turns on her heel and walks back into the living room.

"Wanna go on a field trip with Auntie Lara? I'll buy you ice cream!"

That's all it takes to get Iris's approval. She's jumping and tugging on Lara's sleeve in no time.

"See," Lara mouths at me. "Easy."

I look at Rathgar, eyebrows raised as if to ask, *did you know about this?* He's not wearing the look of utter confusion that I am, but I can't tell much else behind his stoic features.

All right, then. Two can play at that game.

Once the door closes, I round on him and put my hands on my hips. "Dinner, huh? When were you going to tell me about this one?"

Rathgar opens his mouth, then pauses. Rubs the back of his neck. "It's not that big of a deal. Thought you could use a night off, is all."

"Mhmm…" I narrow my eyes, still skeptical. If he has an ulterior motive, he's not showing his hand. Not yet. But my heart skips a beat at the thought of us having a private night together for the first time since the cottages.

Was this his way of asking me on a date?

The words wither on my tongue unsaid. I don't want to rock the boat and assume something I shouldn't. Rathgar is a warrior first, and just like Iris comes first in my life, his duty to his planet and his kin has to come first for him.

On the surface, a pairing like us would never work out. But the more time I spend with him, the more I wonder if the matchmaking system at the ISA knew what it was talking about after all.

Rathgar closes the distance between us and puts one hand on the small of my back, the other right under my chin. My skin prickles at his closeness, my heart speeding up in time with his breaths. His voice, warm and sumptuous, flows over me like honey. "Now how about that dinner?"

I DIDN'T REALIZE how much I needed a night to myself. For so long, I've put myself last. I take care of everything and everyone. It's what I do. It's what I'm good at. But tonight, Rathgar doesn't let me lift a finger.

He puts together a decadent dinner of squid ink pasta and shrimp, topping it off with a fresh salad picked straight from the garden. The airiest, most buttery garlic bread I've ever tasted in my life practically melts in my mouth and we wash it down with fizzy grape juice since I can't have wine. When I think I can't eat another bite, Rathgar takes my plate and goes to clean up before I even have a chance to offer.

What has gotten into him? Whatever it is, I'm not complaining. While he finishes up in the kitchen I move to the bedroom. The word 'nest' is more accurate, actually. I've sectioned off a portion of the room to collect all the most comforting textures, colors, and smells. Everything that makes me feel happy, comfortable, and safe.

It's a great luxury to have the space and resources to do something like this. Back on Earth even having a blanket of my own would have been a tall order. Now here I have a cozy nest filled with all my favorite things, a place to relax, cuddle, and just be.

I sink down into the pile of pillows, cradling my stomach. The baby's growing larger by the day, and they're up and active after the large meal, pressing against my stomach with kicks and flutters that send my heart racing. My eyes droop closed and I pull one of the chunky knit blankets over my lap until I hear his footsteps again.

"You all right in here?" Rathgar peeks into the room. His face lights up when he sees me like this, and the baby must realize he's near as well. Another swift kick and I let out a gasp, hand going to my stomach.

"Rathgar, the baby's kicking. Come here. You can feel it."

For a moment he looks confused. Then worried. "…kicking? Is that good?"

"Yes, it's wonderful. Means they're healthy and happy and learning to move inside of me."

His face goes a little green at the prospect, but I laugh and wave him over again. "It's fine, I promise. Human babies do this all the time in the womb. Come, I want you to feel this."

Rathgar still looks a bit uneasy, but he steps into the room and closes the door. Kneeling next to the nest, he takes my hand and covers it with his own. I'll never get over the warm strength of his palms. The weight of his body next to mine.

"Show me."

I take his hand and position it over my stomach, just in time for another kick. His eyes widen and he nearly jerks his hand away.

"I-incredible..." The look of sheer reverence on his face is not something I'll forget any time soon. He looks like he's just witnessed a miracle.

And honestly, come to think of it? He kind of has.

The circumstances of our mating are a miracle all their own, but when I think about how hard it is for Aesir couples to conceive children, I feel another rush of womanly pride.

"What's the matter?" I say softly, taking my other hand to cup his face.

"Is the big mean warrior at a loss for words?"

Maybe I'm playing with fire, being so forward with him like this. I can blame it on the hormones tomorrow.

But tonight? Maybe I want to get burned.

"Does this answer your question?" His voice comes out raw, loaded with emotion and desire.

With one hand on my stomach, he leans in before covering my mouth with his own. He uses the little gasp of surprise to his advantage, slipping his warm, wet tongue along the crease of my lips before delving inside, deepening the kiss further. My hand drops from his cheek and instead goes to the back of his neck, joining my other hand as I pull him closer.

My body melts into the kiss, all the tension and stress of the recent past dissolving with each second we're glued together. He breaks away, breathing hard, and I make a garbled sort of noise before reaching for him again. "We shouldn't..." I whisper, trying to keep some semblance of rationality. I told myself I wouldn't get attached. That I would only do what was necessary.

So why does having him around feel so right?

"Shouldn't we?" Rathgar rumbles, hot and heavy next to my ear. I shiver at the feel of his breath on my skin. He pulls back just far enough that I can see his eyes and the sincerity behind them. "I know I'm not the perfect man, Janie. I know I make mistakes, and I know you deserve a man who can give you the world. Who can give you more than I ever could..." He trails off, breaking eye contact.

"Rathgar..." Even the sound of his name on my lips triggers something deep in my chest. I reach for him again.

"If you want me to leave..." He starts to sit back up. "If you want me to stop..." Rathgar frowns. Shakes his head. "When I chose to be your alpha, I promised never to hurt you. But what I didn't realize was that making things work with another person is about more than just a contract or a set of rules. It's about trust. And communication. Neither which I've done a stellar job at."

I watch him through tear-blurred eyes. Rathgar, the big bad alpha, was admitting that he did something wrong? I thought I'd never see the day.

"When you disappeared," I say softly, my chest seizing with emotion. "I didn't know what to think. All that kept running through my mind was..." My face darkens as my old memories come and try to spoil this intimate moment. I know that Rathgar is really trying. I try and fail to swallow the lump in my throat. "You know. Before."

Rathgar bows his head. He places his right fist to his chest while holding my hand with the other. "I should never have left my omega alone and in need. I never planned to be gone for so long, but one thing led to another. I was thoughtless. And I was wrong."

It wasn't going to change everything overnight, but the fact that he realized how he'd hurt me meant more than words could say. This time, I'm the one at a loss for words.

"I know I'm not the best man, or the best alpha, or the best mate. I never intended to pair with anyone, much less an omega from Earth. I thought Soren was crazy to even suggest it. But then I met you...and you turned out to be one of the most maddening women I've ever met." He lets out a wistful laugh, and when he looks into my eyes once more, the pure adoration I see there disarms what little defenses I have left.

"I can't promise you that I'll never have to leave again. And I can't promise you that I'll always know the right thing to say or to do. But I can promise that I will protect you and Iris and our baby until my dying day -- if you'll let me."

No one had ever said that to me before. No one had ever cared about me that way or taken the time to put themselves out there. I was always looking after others and putting myself last. But with Rathgar, he makes me feel like a queen. He makes me feel like maybe I am worthy of love after all.

I still think he's a bit of a jerk, and I still worry about the future, but for right now?

I don't need to say another word. With tears in my eyes, I pull him into my nest as he kisses me.

THE FIRST FEW — or first few dozen — times we had sex when I was in heat, we were driven by nothing more than pure animal need. We couldn't keep our hands off of one another and our sex reflected that: raw, passionate, and smoking hot.

But as we undress each other in the soft comfort of my nest, this is something else altogether. The way his touches linger on my skin and leave a trail of heat in their wake. The reverent way he says my name and caresses my swollen belly. And even in the way I react to him as well, wrapping my arms around him so tight and drawing in his scent, afraid to let him go.

He whispers my name over and over like a prayer, peppering me with kisses and slow, languid thrusts that make me see stars. The brutal edge has all but vanished, leaving in its place a warm, caring man who simply wants to make me happy.

It feels too good to be true, but when I come apart on his cock and tears flow from my eyes at last, I'm afraid to consider otherwise. As I drift into a peaceful sleep, wrapped in my carefully prepared nest and in Rathgar's loving arms, I realize I could get used to this. I'm afraid.

GIFTED NUTCRACKER

RATHGAR

It's only two days later when I receive a summons from Soren. He's gathering all the alphas together in the meeting hall. Says it's important.

And it's like my worst fear coming true. I'm finally starting to have a breakthrough with Janie. Starting to get her to trust me. And starting to feel my own heart open as well. It's more exhilarating and more terrifying than any battle, and if I have to leave again…

It could undo everything I've worked so hard to build.

A battle of wills plays out in my conflicted brain when I step into the meeting hall and see all of them there. Soren sits at the head of the table and nods at me as I enter. I'm the last one there; I take my seat to Soren's right, bracing myself for what happens next.

"Alphas of Aesirheim," Soren booms. His sonorous voice carries well past the gathering of a dozen or so men. It bounces off the walls and seems to go on forever. "We've received word of an…anomaly, for lack of a better word. Normally docile creatures are attacking villagers right outside our borders. They're on the move, and we've lost contact with our away teams. That's why I've called you all here."

My heart rate shoots up, the familiar rush of adrenaline and battle spirit flowing through my veins. Normally, I'd be the first to jump on an opportunity like this. But a stone of dread settles in the pit of my stomach. What about Janie? What about Iris?

And most of all, what about our child?

It's not just me that I have to worry about anymore. Whether she accepts me fully as her mate or not, I made her a promise. And to betray that trust would be the very antithesis of all I hold dear.

"We need volunteers to go investigate the source of the disturbance and bring our men home." He glances over at me as he says it, seemingly reading my thoughts. "Sitting in this room are the best trackers, warriors, and healers that Aesirheim has to offer. And if we fail to act now, if we let this threat continue unchecked, we could be next." His throat bobs with emotion. "Our families could be next."

I shift in my seat, fists clamping the arms of the chair in a death grip. This is what I signed up for, so long ago. To protect and serve the people of Aesirheim from any and all threats, external and internal. I took an oath, and I took it yet further when I elected to be part of the first test group for the Alpha Project.

I dedicated my life and my body to protecting our planet and our people. And that, I realize with a shiver, now includes Janie.

While the other alphas talk among themselves, Soren gestures to me to follow him. "May I speak with you privately?"

This can't be good. "Coming."

We step into a side room and Soren looks me up and down, a knowing expression on his face. "I know we just had this discussion about you and Janie, so if you aren't able to make it…" He trails off. "You know I wouldn't call you here unless I really needed you. Unless Aesirheim needed you." He averts his gaze, looking past me. "I'll give you leave, just this once. All you have to do is say the word."

It should have been easy. To thank him for his generosity and go back home where my mate and children were waiting.

But I made a promise to myself, and a promise to the planet. I would not stand down in the face of danger now. "I'll do it." I say softly. "I'll go with you."

Soren perks up. "Are you sure?"

I give a quick nod before I can change my mind. "Yes."

"Very well." Before snapping back into commander mode, he looks at me sidelong, a hint of mischief sparkling there. "And you know, there is one perk to going out on these away missions…"

"Oh?"

Soren's wolflike grin spreads across his whole face. "Let's just say that Lara is *very* happy to see me when I return, if you know what I mean."

I open my mouth to respond, but my face heats up as I realize the implication of his words. I hadn't even thought about that, but now that he mentioned it…

I could get the thrill of battle, bring back a trophy for Janie, maybe a skin to use as a blanket for the new baby. All that *and* the thought of her jumping my bones the minute I get in the door?

"Welcome to the team," Soren says with a wink, and we go to join the others once more.

* * *

EVEN THOUGH I know its necessary, I'm not excited about telling Janie I'll have to leave again. If we're lucky, it won't be long and I'll be in her arms again before I know it.

If we're not lucky…I'm not even going to think about it.

On my way back to our house I pick up Janie's favorite snack. The pregnancy cravings have mostly subsided, but I can't go a day without hearing her talk about hafta nuts. She tried them for the first time when Iris got into my duffel bag and started pulling out random things. Ever since then, she's been hooked on the unique salty and savory flavor.

It's not much of a peace offering, but I want to remember the look of joy and gratitude on her face. I want to fix it in my mind and my memory so that she's never far away.

That, and she's eating for two, after all. What kind of alpha would I be if I didn't feed my hungry omega?

"I'm home!" I call as I push open the door and step inside. Janie's reclining on the couch watching something on her tablet while Iris sleeps next to her. One hand holds her tablet aloft while the other cradles her pregnant belly. My heart pangs and softens again at the sight of the child's small, sleeping body. Not to mention the little one growing inside of Janie.

For their sake, I have to fight. I have to do this.

Janie looks up, her face breaking into a smile. "Welcome back," she says. "Everything all right? I know you rushed out in a hurry."

My face darkens, throat closing for a second. She wastes no time getting to the point — never has.

But I'm an alpha warrior of Aesirheim, second only to Soren himself. I will not stand down. "There's something I need to talk to you about," I say carefully, sitting down on the remaining edge of the couch.

I hate the way her face instantly morphs into concern, then fear. "What's wrong?" Even her voice loses the cheer it had only moments ago. I hate this. I hate all of this. But I remind myself — and I'll remind her — that it's for us. For our future. Together.

"Remember when I left the last time?" There's no easy way to say this.

Her frown deepens; she shifts to sit up straighter. Iris, for her part, stays fast asleep — for now. "Yeah…?"

I draw my bottom lip between my teeth before huffing out a breath and steeling myself. "There have been attacks, and they're getting closer. Soren needs us to go and stamp them out before they get any closer." I rub the back of my neck, knowing how she's going to take it. "Soren's going, too, if that makes you feel any better."

Janie stays still for a moment, lips parted only slightly in question, eyes wide and confused. Then it dawns on her. The emotion and the pain visibly washes over her body like the darkness of a thunderstorm. She looks away from me and over to Iris instead. But even from this angle, I can see the tears at the corner of her eyes. Can see the taut line of her jaw, trying to hold back the tide.

Iris stirs, blinking open groggy eyes. When she rolls over, she sees me sitting there and raises a hand to wave at me. At least she's still smiling. "Rahrah," she mutters sleepily.

Stars, this is hard. I knew it would be difficult to leave her again, especially with her advancing pregnancy and my advancing feelings, but the look on her broken face and Iris's sweet, innocent expression gut me deeper than any sword.

"You're leaving again." Janie's voice is flat. Final. It's not a question.

"Yes," I say with a sigh. "But I don't want to keep you in the dark, Janie. Not like last time."

"You said…" She whispers. A single tear falls and she sniffs, swiping it away before turning her head.

"I know." And she's right. There's nothing I can say to magically make it better. That's what makes this the hardest part of all. "If I had any other choice…"

Janie shrugs. She bends down and picks up Iris, cradling her in her lap. Iris clings to her chest and makes my heart ache even more. "Soren has to leave Lara sometimes too, you know. They've made it work. You know your sister better than I do. Maybe you could talk to her about it."

She doesn't answer for a long while. Maybe she wants me to leave. Maybe she doesn't want to talk to me anymore. I'm about to throw in the towel and turn away when she speaks again. "How long?"

More uncertainty. More disappointing non-answers. "I won't be long. And Soren's got a private comms line. You'll know if anything changes."

She's still frowning, but her demeanor lightens a bit. "I'll be back before you know it," I promise, taking her hand. "I meant what I said the other night." I press a soft kiss to her knuckles. "I've got to go, but I'm not leaving. I'm not leaving you, Janie. And I'm not leaving Iris, and I'm not leaving our child. I will be back. I swear to you."

Another stray tear falls, but she nods and squeezes my hand. "Be safe."

"I will," I promise, leaning forward to kiss her forehead.

"Rah-rah?" Iris cranes her head to look at me, her face crumpled in confusion. "What about the monsters under the bed?"

Ah. That. It had become something of our little tradition in the short time I'd spent with Iris and Janie. Now that Iris had her own bedroom and bed, she was quite adamant about 'protecting' it.

Just like her mother.

One night she came into our room crying, talking about a monster under the bed and saying she couldn't sleep. I did what any alpha — no, any *dad* — would do.

I took out my weapon and let her watch me scout through the room, making a show of looking in all the nooks and crannies. I told her I scared the monster off, and he wouldn't try anything while I was around. It was a small thing, but the look of sheer admiration in her eyes is one I'll never forget.

She acted like I was her hero in that moment, and I guess I was. So every night, before she went to bed, I'd go into the room and 'fight off' anything that might be lurking before I tucked her in. She loved it, and I enjoyed it more than I thought I would as well.

But now I was leaving, and both she — and Janie — would have to face the monsters on their own. Both literally and figuratively.

I reach into my belt and pull out a small, thin tool I use mostly for cracking the hafta nuts Janie likes so much. To the outside observer, it almost looks like a tiny knife — only, the sharp edges are all on the inside.

"Rah-rah's gotta go for a few days." I crouch down to eye level and meet her worried gaze. "But I'm leaving this with you, okay? Can you take care of it for me?"

"A present?" Iris tilts her head.

"Something like that." I smile. "Hold out your hand."

Iris extends her palm and I give her the small tool. She looks upon it with awe, gripping it tightly in her small fingers.

"Can you be a big girl for me while I'm gone?" The words dredge up that sad, forgotten emotion in my chest all over again. Her eyes, shiny and scared, never leave mine.

"I'll try." Holding up the nutcracker, she says, "Will this keep the monsters away?"

I nod. "Keep it right next to your bed, okay? It will make sure no one bothers you while I'm gone. And if you get scared in the middle of the night, you grab it and it will keep you safe." I take the hand that's not holding the nutcracker and clasp it in my own, giving it a small squeeze. "I'll be back soon. I promise."

Iris sniffs back a tear and holds the nutcracker to her chest. "Okay. Miss you."

Oof. Another shot to the heart. I always thought it was impossible to miss someone before they're even gone. I was wrong.

Turning back to Janie, she has the most curious expression on her face. The fear's still there, but there's a soft, caring undercurrent that permeates everything.

"Thank you," she whispers. "Iris will remember that." She folds her hands over her belly. "I'll remember that."

"It's the least I can do."

"Just…" Her voice wavers, as if she's unsure what she wants to say next. "Come home safe."

I wrap my arms around her and pull her close. I want to remember this feeling. I won't let this be a repeat of last time. This time, I am not leaving as a method of getting away.

I'm leaving *because* I have something worth fighting for.

After a long moment, I pull away, pressing a kiss to her belly and then giving Iris a long, comforting hug. She clings to me even longer than Janie. When I break away at last, she's still clutching the tool — the 'weapon' — I gave her to her chest like a precious treasure.

I know if I stay here much longer, I'll crack. So with one last look and a hand raised in farewell, I grab my duffel and head to the meeting point.

I'll come back to you, Janie. I'll prove it to you, and Iris, and everyone. I'm tired of running. I will do everything I can to be the man, the alpha, and the father you need.

RAIDED HOME

JANIE

I know this time is different, but it still doesn't make the house feel any less empty. It still doesn't make me feel any less alone.

This time I opt to stay in Rathgar's house with Iris. We settled into the place nicely, and he really did put a lot of thought into making sure we were comfortable.

Rathgar's house. The thought passes and I amend it with a smile.

No, our *house.*

The thought fills me with a sense of pride for once in my life. Of belonging. The future, with all its uncertainty, looms before us. I still don't know what will happen to Rathgar and I over the long term. We've grown closer, and Iris positively adores him, but actually marrying the man? Making a real life together with the three — no, the four of us?

I just don't know.

So it's with those thoughts in mind that I'm lying awake in the middle of the night, curled up in my nest and gazing out the window at the stars above.

I wonder where he is right now. I wonder what he's doing. If he's thinking of me.

I hear a knock on the door and I jump, before hearing Iris's soft voice on the other side. "Mommy?"

"What is it, sweetheart?"

"I can't sleep. Can I stay with you?"

I get up and open the door to find her standing there in her nightgown, holding her stuffed bunny in one hand and rubbing her eyes with the other. How could I say no to that face?

"Of course. Why don't you come in here and get comfy."

She crawls into the nest and burrows under the blankets, instantly looking more at ease. I can't blame her — the nest has a soothing effect on me, too. But I'm still not used to sleeping alone after spending time with Rathgar. Somewhere along the way, I not only got used to his body pressed against mine as I slept, but I came to expect it.

To need it, even.

Now he wasn't here, and no matter how I tossed and turned, I couldn't stop thinking about him. Maybe Iris was feeling the same.

With her curled up in bed next to me, my anxiety slows down to a dull roar. Soon enough, I hear the soft sounds of her breathing as she falls asleep, and it's not long before I do the same.

THE SOUND of splintering wood forces me awake, all grogginess gone in a matter of seconds. Iris jerks up as well, wailing and burying herself in my arms. Shouts, screams, angry voices. My heart leaps into my throat.

I glance at the door then back at the window. I have no idea what time it is, but it's still dark. That is, it would be if not for the flames right outside my window.

With a shriek, I leap out of bed, mind racing. What was going on? Rathgar, Soren, and several of the other alphas were gone, but that didn't leave us completely unprotected, right?

Iris continues to wail and I look around the room for something, anything I can use to ward off the attackers. It's not much of a plan, especially since I'm not only much weaker than any Aesir man or woman, but I'm also pregnant. But my maternal instincts kick into overdrive and I have to do something.

We can't get out the window — the flames are too close. Oh God, what about Lara? Was she okay? What about Ray?

The shouts grow closer and stomping footsteps join them. The splintering sound booms through the house again and this time I have to cover my mouth to hold in a scream. Someone was breaking in!

"Mommy!" Iris wails, clinging to my side. There's no way out, but I can't have them getting in here, either. I need to buy time. I need to do something…

Grabbing the chair Rathgar uses for his desk, I throw it in front of the bedroom door. "Mommy, what's happening?" Iris cries. I know she's scared and I know she can't help it, but there's no way we're going to stay hidden like this.

There's only one choice.

We'll have to fight.

"It's okay, sweetheart." I mutter over and over, trying to soothe her cries. "Mommy's here, Mommy's got you." All the while, I'm scrambling, picking through the dresser, looking for anything that might help us. Yanking open Soren's desk drawer I spot the letter opener and grab it, brandishing it like a knife. It's a pitiful weapon, especially against a fully armed intruder, but it's all I have.

And if this is how I'm going to go out, I will not go quietly.

"Shhh," I whisper to Iris, holding a finger to my lips. "Get behind me." She whimpers once more and sniffs, rubbing her eyes.

I hold my breath, straining to listen for any words or names I might recognize. Nothing. Then, just like before, the walls and floor shake with impact and the door flies open, the huge silhouette of our attacker looming in the doorway.

To my credit, I don't scream. There's a little whimper in the back of my throat and I'm shaking like crazy, but I don't cry. I don't scream. If I hadn't been going to the bathroom nonstop due to pregnancy belly, I would have wet my pants.

Holding the letter opener out in front of me with both shaking hands, I try to take in the brute of a man before me. He's nearly as large as Soren and Rathgar, but thicker around the middle and with legs like tree trunks. His face has a long scar across one eye, and the tendons on his neck stick out with rage or excitement, I can't tell.

"What are you doing here?" Somehow, I manage to keep my voice fairly calm. I'm praying against all hope that they won't notice Iris. That they won't hurt her. I'll die before that happens.

"What's it look like, missy? Those fools finally fell for it. This is a raid."

My stomach turns over. A raid. Oh god. Here?!

"You don't know what you're getting yourself into." I try to sound intimidating, but its not like a pregnant human woman with a letter opener is any match for their sheer bulk and brutality. "Don't you know who owns these lands? When they find out what you've done, there will be no mercy."

"Oh, I'm well aware…" He says in a sickly sweet tone that makes my skin crawl. "And that's exactly why we're here. Now you're coming with me — the easy way, or the hard way."

"No!" Iris cries, jumping out from behind my leg. "Don't take my mommy!"

So much for keeping her hidden. The grim reality of our situation sets in and my stomach turns again, bile building at the back of my throat. I know enough from Soren and Rathgar's war stories to know what happens next.

"Mommy, huh?" The intruder looks genuinely surprised. "Well, aren't you just the sweetest thing." He rakes his eyes up and down my body before lingering on my rounded belly. "Looks like someone's been busy."

Red-hot anger explodes in my chest and I clench my jaw. "Get. Out."

"Sorry, princess, but that ain't happening. I'll start with the little one, and if you want her to see the next sunrise, you'll do as I say."

Now it was my turn to scream. "No!" The word wrenches itself from my throat and I lunge forward to grab at Iris, but he's too fast. He hauls her up and over his shoulder, ignoring her terrified pleas for help. "Give her back!" I yell, rushing after him. "You bastard! Take me instead, just please, don't hurt my baby!"

"Oh, two birds with one stone?" He chuckles. "Don't mind if I do."

And right when I've closed the distance between us, right when Iris's fingers are only a second away, another man steps out of the shadows, wrapping a strong arm around my throat and cutting off my line of sight.

I try to kick, to scream, to do something and get someone's attention, but it's no use. I hear my daughter's cries, but everything's so muddled. I can't see straight and the man holding me has his rough, smelly hand pressed over my face and throat. "No!" I scream again as something rough — a hood with soporific chemicals in it, perhaps? — settles over my head. He's dragging me along, my feet barely touching the floor. A rush of cool air means we're outside, and the stench hits me like a truck.

I gag. Luckily nothing comes up. And just before everything goes black, I hear one more familiar voice, putting the final nail in the proverbial cauldron.

Lara.

They've got her too.

So where was everyone else? How had they managed to ambush us so easily? And as my captor's rough hand leads me, bound and blindfolded, away from my home, my heart cries out for only one thing:

Rathgar, wherever you are...come back soon. Please. Hurry. I need you.

SMOLDERING REMAINS

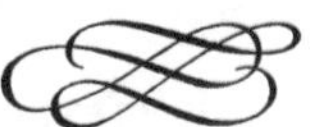

RATHGAR

Something's not right. And I don't just mean the miscommunication by the field team. We geared up for what sounded like, by all reports, a serious battle. Imagine our surprise — and confusion — when we got to the waypoint only to find that our scouts were alive and well.

That was the first mistake. We did manage to track down the roving creatures, but even they weren't as much of a threat as we first thought. With the situation wrapped up in record time, we're regrouping and preparing to head home early when I turn to Soren, unable to hold in my question any longer.

"It's not like you to get bad intel." I'm throwing my pack over my aki, trying not to sound too accusatory. "Thought it was gonna be a bloodbath."

"I'm just as concerned as you are, Rathgar." He secures his pack and climbs onto his mount, turning her back toward the shuttle. "There's something that doesn't fit here. Something I'm missing. But for the life of me, I can't figure out what."

"I know the feeling," I mutter, and for a time, we travel in silence. So what *is* that nagging feeling in my gut? I try to ignore it, writing it off as nerves, but it grows stronger the closer we get to the shuttle. Soren's feeling it too, I can tell. Even his aki, Caltryx, walks with a tense and restless gait.

The wind blows in from the nearby mountains, and on the breeze I could swear I heard a familiar voice.

Janie's voice.

I guess I really am losing it.

But right then, Soren snaps to attention as well. The change is instantaneous — from slightly confused to utterly horrified and then to murderously furious. "Rathgar! The women!"

He spurs his mount into a gallop and I rush to keep up, my heart thundering in time with each hoof beat. It couldn't be. Couldn't be…

"What's wrong?" I yell when I catch up. I've only seen him like this once before, and that's when his heart-mate Lara had to leave Aesirheim to take care of her sister after she was injured. The fear I tried to put aside rises to the fore all over again. I wasn't imagining things. Something had happened. Even I could feel it.

"It's Lara," Soren pants, rushing toward the shuttle at breakneck speed. "It was a trap, this whole setup was a trap. There was an ambush back home. We were fools, Rathgar. Fools!"

Equal parts terror and fury wash over me like a storm. All the rest of the world fades away, sounds and sensations easing into the background as my thoughts and energy redirect to one purpose and one purpose only:

Saving my mate.

WE MAKE it home in record time, but it's too late. Charred remains smolder against the once-lush landscape. It's a bleak picture compared to the thriving community we left, but now it's like a ghost town.

"Janie!" I cry out when I see our house still standing but damaged. The door hangs weakly on its destroyed hinges. Shattered glass litters the ground where the windows broke and sharp splinters poke out from the wooden frame. If something happened to her and the kids –

No force in the galaxy will stop me from taking my revenge.

"Janie!" I roar again, praying that I'll hear her voice. That she will be there, with that same soft smile on her face. That Iris will wake up next to her and cry out to me with that endearing nickname of hers.

But the house stands ransacked and empty. My blood runs hotter with each room I check. My rage fuels my movements, clouding out everything else. The last room I check is our bedroom. Janie's nest.

The door's destroyed here too, but there's signs of a struggle. Did my omega actually try to fight them off? I should never have left her, and the fact that they stooped so low as to abduct a child…

Mark my words. When I find the bastards that did this, they will regret ever crossing an Aesirheim Alpha.

I turn to leave, wild with panic and rage, until something smeared across the wood catches my eye. I freeze at first, thinking that it is blood, but a closer inspection reveals the truth.

It's paint. Red face paint.

The very same that Kovarx's men use in the field.

A cold, grisly certainty fills my chest and I let out a loud, mournful roar that shakes the still-standing timbers. Memories of his threat come back to me in full color, remembering all too well his crimes and his vow for revenge.

I should have killed the bastard when I had the chance, after I saw what he had done to his own wife and child. Should have tossed him from the tower and watched as he splattered into a pulp on the cobblestones. I showed a rare moment of mercy, and this is what I got.

When I find him again, he will not be so lucky.

I will make him pay for every breath, every life he's stolen here today. When

I'm finished with him, not even the crows will want his corpse.

Everything's a blur after that. I rush back out into the main square, where Soren's just as unhinged as I am.

"They took her." I spit, snarling at the scorched ground. "Taking a pregnant omega, and her child, too…" My fists clench so tightly my nails dig into the skin. "The monsters!"

"Got any leads?" Soren's voice is low, monotone. Deadly.

"I do." I say. And this time, with all the might of Aesirheim behind us, we will not fail. We cannot afford to fail our women and children. There is no cost too high to pay to get them back.

IMPRISONED IN A CELL

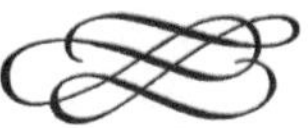

JANIE

I heard stories of alien brutality in passing from listening to Soren's old war stories. I never thought I would be part of one.

I'm sitting in a dank cell with Iris, Lara, and one other woman. She's human like us, just moved in with her match not long ago. Isabella, I think she said her name was.

I'm barefoot and pregnant — literally — in a smelly prison cell, but Isabella's got it even worse. We learn amidst sobs that her alpha mate fought valiantly to protect her as one of the few remaining warriors, but ultimately the attackers overwhelmed him. He was slaughtered before her eyes.

All while she was still in heat.

I remember all too vividly how uncomfortable and all-consuming it was, and that was in the lap of luxury with my alpha at my side. The chaos and terror of our situation keeps most of the stronger effects at bay, but she's sweaty, grieving, and in pain. There's only so much we can do.

After the first few hours, Iris finally cried herself out and fell asleep in my arms. At least they didn't separate us. At least Lara is still here as well. I try to remind myself of the positive notes to keep myself from spiraling into panic, but…

Let's be real. I've been kidnapped by alien savages. There's nothing positive about it.

One tiny sliver of good news — if you can call it that — is that Ray was off with one of Soren's friends on a mini field trip of sorts. They were well out of range when the raid happened, but what would they think when they returned home to see everyone gone?

Lara promises me that Ray's all right. I asked her how she knows, and apparently that's a feature of having a child with your 'heart-mate'. Just as she can feel Soren's presence, even over lightyears of distance, she too can sense her son's life force. I can only imagine what could have happened if he'd been there when the raiders attacked.

I have no way to know how much time has passed. I only know that I'm hungry, sore, and scared for my life. Lara's doing her best to look after Isabella and giving the death glare to any guard who comes by and lingers on her a little too long, but there's not much we can physically do.

Please, Rathgar. Where are you?

Despair starts to seep in, little by little. It's only a trickle at first, like an occasional drip from a leaky faucet. But the more time that passes, the more Iris cries and the more Isabella wails and the more I sit here in this dark, timeless void, the more doubt creeps in. A tiny drip turns into a trickle, and then a small stream.

He probably doesn't even know where we are. And if he does, will they make it here in time?

Another loud crash. I should be getting used to loud crashes by now, but every one makes me jump. Makes me hold Iris just a little bit closer. She's not the only one that's terrified. Even my baby seems to know what's up, moving and shifting and pressing against all the wrong spots. I should be resting and taking it easy.

Instead, I'm in a literal cage while some alien brute decides what to do with me.

"Soren will come," Lara promises me, but it sounds more like she's trying to convince herself. "He will. Rathgar too. They'll find us. We'll be fine. We'll be fine."

But the way she hugs her knees to her chest, the way she fusses over Isabella, and the way silent tears fall when she thinks I'm not looking tell me things aren't fine at all.

I would say we've been through worse, but poverty and starvation is one thing. Being literally kidnapped and our lives threatened by a violent group of hostile aliens is quite another.

Time bleeds together into one hazy, painful fever dream. I don't know what time it is or how long its been. I'm drifting in and out of sleep when the sound of footsteps rouses me.

"Rathgar?" My body jerks upright and my heart skips a beat. The fact that he was the first word on my lips tells all. But when the silhouette comes into view, it's not Rathgar at all. It's worse.

While Soren and Rathgar have bulky, imposing builds that show off their muscles and sheer physical power, this man looks like some kind of experiment gone wrong. His proportions are all over the place, and the only thing that's consistent about him are the haggard scars etching just about every inch of his body. His dark, beady eyes fixate on me. A sick grin crawls up his face; I cringe away on instinct, but there's nowhere to go.

His filthy gaze crawls up and down my body, and I swear I can feel it on me like a spider. Iris, for her part, hasn't woken up yet. Good. She doesn't need to see this.

"Knock knock." He raps on the bars of the cell with one grimy hand. Even his voice makes my stomach churn. If my stomach wasn't so empty, I would have hurled. "How are my guests doing?"

All I can do is snarl.

"But where are my manners? My name is Kovarx. What's yours?"

I don't meet his gaze. I don't say a word. I'm not going to cooperate with a villain like him.

"Oh, giving me the silent treatment?" He makes a tsk sound with his tongue, and there's a flash of panic. Was he going to punish me now? "That's all right. I don't need to know your name to know who you are."

With a flash of movement, he leans inward, his face reaching through the bars. He's even more hideous up close, and I can see the sweat and grime sticking to his skin. Just that's enough to make me want to gag. "You're one of his." He rasps. "I can smell it all over you."

My blood turns to ice just as my baby kicks again. I hiss in a shattered breath, holding my stomach. "You don't know what you've gotten yourself into," I growl through clenched teeth. "Rathgar will come, and when he does I'll delight in watching him destroy you."

"So confident, are we? But you see, it was I who orchestrated that little diversion in the first place. They will be far afield by now, and even if they do come back?" His eyes flash with murderous glee. "They'll be too late."

Equal parts rage and panic well up inside of me. I take what energy I have left and spit, right at his feet. I know I'm playing with fire, but I'm too mad to care. The longer I can keep him talking, the longer I can string this along, the more time Soren and

Rathgar have to arrive. I just need to hold out a little longer.

Kovarx doesn't take kindly to my display of disgust. With a quick, harsh movement that belies his huge size, he grabs me from inside the cell, yanking me to the front. My joints cry out. I scream and kick, trying anything I can to get away from him. But it's no use. He's too strong, and he's got two misshapen cronies guarding the cell right next to the doorway.

Iris is awake now, held firmly in Lara's arms while she looks on, a scream building on her lips.

"Mama!" Iris cries out for me, and the last thing I remember as they drag me away is a cold, resigned conviction. If this was going to be the end for me, I'd at least give Lara, Iris, and Isabella all the time I could.

I never wanted to give my heart to Rathgar. I never wanted to give my heart to any man after what happened with my old flame back on Earth. But as I'm dragged away from my family, I realize that I unwillingly already have.

Rathgar is my heart-mate. But will I live long enough to tell him the truth?

TEAM'S RESCUE

RATHGAR

I should have killed the bastard when I had a chance. But I let myself get soft, and now Janie was in danger because of me. That's not a mistake I plan to make twice.

With my tracking skills and Soren's resources, we were able to sniff out his hideout pretty easily. I don't know how he got out of that locked room I left him in, but it doesn't matter. I'm done seeing him slip through my fingers. This time, I will not leave until he's dead.

We're circling Kovarx's camp, just the two of us with two other alpha scouts. We can't afford tipping them off to our presence. We have to be quick, quiet, and deadly.

My specialty.

I hold back a yawn as Soren points at something over the hill we're stationed on. I haven't had more than a few minutes of shut eye since Soren first got the news that something was wrong. But that's all right. I've been through much worse conditions in the field. It's not the first time I've had to sacrifice sleep for the sake of my duty, or the sake of my people.

It's not just 'your people' anymore, I remind myself. It still feels so strange. So foreign. But in a good way. A way I never thought I'd be able to claim for myself. *Your family.*

A soft breeze stirs the grass and blows my sweaty hair out of my face. That's not all it does, though. I catch a whiff of something all too familiar — the very scent that had me rushing through the ISA facility to find her that fateful day.

It's Janie. She's here.

And she's terrified.

Soren notices me tense up. "I know," he says softly. "I smell them too. But we can't be hasty."

"Easy for you to say," I grumble. My skin itches all over, my heart pounding in my chest. I need to punch something. I need to scream. And more than anything, I need to hold Janie and Iris in my arms and make sure nothing will ever hurt them again.

"I know," Soren says again. He looks almost as tense as I do, but he's better at hiding. A vein pops out on his forehead, ticking in time with his sped-up heart. "I feel it too, believe me. It's taking everything I have to keep from storming in there like the beasts they think we are."

I dig my fingers into the grass and try to ground myself. Letting out a long breath, I nod my head. "What's our next move?"

"See that building?" Soren points again. "That's our target. They're in there. I know it."

"Then what are we waiting for? Let's go!"

He holds up a hand. "Not yet. They'll be changing the guard soon. Orri and Ivar are scouting the perimeter now. When I get the signal, we're clear to proceed."

I grunt out an acknowledgement, but my brain's still elsewhere. Thinking of Janie and Iris, alone and scared. The fact that they took Janie and Lara was bad enough. But to put a child — no, a *toddler* — through this?

Unforgivable.

A few more moments pass. I stare at the compound, but can't see a thing. Finally, Soren nudges me. "Let's go." He checks his weapon one more time, holds a finger to his lips, and we're off down the hill. When this is all over, either Kovarx will be dead…

Or I will be.

By all the gods. I knew that Kovarx and his men were vile, but this…

This is another level.

We get in the door without incident, but there at the long of a long hallway is an utter cage. And there, wailing for her mommy, is Iris.

At that point, nothing Soren says can stop me anymore. There's a man guarding the cell with his back turned, but he won't be there for long. He doesn't even deserve to be called a man.

I rush toward him, drawing my sword as I go, and before he even has a chance to turn around, I slit the bastard's throat and let him fall, wordlessly, to the floor in a wet splatter. His blood coats my blade and my skin, but my thoughts are on something else.

Lara rouses into consciousness, staring at me with wide eyes. Even Iris stops crying. There's another woman there, too. One I haven't seen before. But over the scent of Iris and Janie — where the hell is Janie? — I smell something else. Omega heat.

And it's coming from the small creature curled up in the fetal position next to them.

Almost on instinct, my brain switches into battle mode. I push aside the pain and terror of seeing Iris and Lara like this. I file away the confusion and the aching, gnawing *need* to drop everything and everyone else in my search for Janie. I'll find her. I will. But first I have to save the people in front of me.

Crouching down, I rustle through the fallen guard's belongings. He's stopped moving at this point, but everything's sticky and covered with blood. No matter. Keys still work no matter how bloody they are.

Finally I find a keycard shoved into a secret pocket of his pants and practically rip the seam trying to get it out. Swiping it through the lock, I thank my lucky stars that it unlocks with only a small hiss and not a grating, rusty jangle.

I check over my shoulder once more. Ivar's there helping Soren move the fallen guard's body, while Orri's standing there, transfixed, at the woman in the cage.

I don't have time for this. I yank open the door and Iris runs to me with arms outstretched. "Dada!" She yells, and for a moment, all the world stops turning.

This child — this little one who I'd had the pleasure to get to know over the last several months — was calling me dada. She'd gone from being afraid but curious at first, and now she was reaching up to me with tearful, awestruck eyes. We're still in danger and I'm surprised we haven't triggered any alarms yet, but I wrap Iris in my arms and kiss the top of her head. Her soft, sweet scent softens the edges of anxiety.

My heart swells despite the adrenaline and fear, and I know in my heart what I've suspected all along. Iris and Janie — they're it for me. I don't care who Iris's deadbeat father is. Iris is MY little girl, and Janie is *my* heart-mate. There's no other way around it.

That realization gives me courage, and I look up to Lara for answers.

She looks dirty and exhausted, but not injured from what I can tell. Hopefully that means the same for Janie, but since she's not here…

Lara's face blanches. "He took Janie," she says, her voice a hoarse whisper. "Find her. We'll go with the others."

My heart skips a beat, battle rage threatening to break free once more. That bastard really wanted to get under my skin, didn't he?

He chose the wrong day to fuck with an Aesirheim Alpha.

I hug Iris close to me one more time, letting the feel of her soft skin give me strength. "You've been so brave, baby girl. So brave." I kiss her forehead and check for injuries — thankfully, she seems fine. Just frightened. "Can you be brave for me while I go get your mommy?" I glance up at Lara, and she gives a curt nod in response. "I'll be right back. I'm gonna go get mommy back from the monster, okay?"

"Okay," her small voice lingers in my head. "R-Rathgar."

First Dada. Now my name.

Yeah, there's no way I'm letting this little girl go.

Soren appears at my side; I hand off Iris to Lara while he helps the both of them out of the cell. Orri's snapped back to reality, and my attention returns to the small, curled-up woman on the cage floor.

"She's in heat," Lara informs me, voice low. "Her mate..." Her voice breaks and she can't finish the sentence. "Please, she can't stay here, but she's having trouble walking, and..."

"I'll take care of her." Orri's voice startles me. He swoops up the half-conscious woman in his arms and with both of them heading for the exit, I set my sights on the final destination.

Kovarx...and Janie.

SLAYING THE VILLAIN

JANIE

"You don't get it, do you?"

Whoever this man is, he really loves hearing himself talk. He's been monologuing ever since they shoved me into this small, concrete room with him.

But talk is a lot safer than the alternative, and if I can just keep him going long enough…

"No, I guess I don't." I try to give him my best doe eyes. Making him think he has the upper hand. Making him think I'll do whatever he says.

I may be a woman and I may be of Earth, but I'm not new to dealing with jerks. It's all about their ego, in the end. But this is more than just a random dude catcalling me or getting a little too handsy after a few drinks.

Not only is my life on the line, but Iris's is, as well. And, I realize with a sickening shudder, so is my unborn baby.

I'm sitting in a flimsy folding chair like a prisoner on some kind of crime show. My wrists are bound and my stomach aches and cramps along with the rest of my muscles, and I try to offer the baby a silent apology.

When they dragged me away, a cold determination set in on top of the fear. I may be a captive of one of the most notorious aliens in the world, but I will not bow to him. I will do my best to be brave. I will uphold my honor, just as Soren and his fellow alphas would in the face of danger.

He can — and probably will — hurt me. But the longer I play to his ego, the longer I keep him talking…

The longer I can stay alive. And the longer the alphas have to get here.

"I am Kovarx Car'Thallan," he says again, as if I'm supposed to be impressed. "And your little 'alphas' fell right into my trap." He makes air quotes with a snarl. What was he talking about?

"Yes, yes, I planned this." He lets out a low chuckle; if I had anything left in my stomach, it would have come up. All I get is a burning sensation in the back of my throat. "After they so foolishly left me during our last meeting, I bet they thought they'd taken the high road. Left me to rot instead of doing the killing themselves, hm?" Kovarx circles around my chair till he's standing behind me. One finger trails over my shoulder and down my arm, and I'm powerless to resist.

I would scream, but who would even hear? I was alone. Just like I'd always been.

My heart skipped at beat at the thought, and at first I thought it was just my nerves. But no, something happened just then when I thought of Rathgar's face. Of his warm embrace, and the soft smile he reserved for Iris only. It was like someone'd lit a candle right in the middle of my chest, and the warmth spread outward, suffusing everything.

"After your so-called alpha — Rathgar, was it? — stole my woman and off-spring away from me, I figured it was only fair that I repay the favor in kind." His breath whispered against my ear. I cringed away, skin crawling, but it wasn't enough.

"Now just what shall I do with — "

A sudden siren cuts off his words, a red light above the door flashing. My heart leaps into my throat — was that them? Were they here?

Kovarx curses furiously and wastes no time hauling me out of the chair. "Looks like we've got company. Isn't that nice? Too bad they'll be too late. Again." And as he yanks me toward the door, he presses a nondescript button on a side panel.

There's no point in trying to keep quiet any longer. This guy was crazy, and he was going to bring the whole building down with him! I scream as loud as I can, my voice cracking and burning my throat.

"Rathgar!" I scream so hard my voice gives out. "Soren! Help!"

His dirty, greasy palm wraps around my neck and covers my mouth. I try and kick backward as hard as I can, hoping to hit his sensitive parts, but I'm too disoriented and miss.

"Self-destruct sequence initiated. Execution in 90 seconds…89…88…"

"No!" I scream one last time. Tears run down my face. Everything hurts. Memories of everything I've been through flash before my eyes, and for a moment I think this really is the end.

I'm sorry, Iris.

"Time to go, sweetheart."

Kovarx stuffs a gross red rag into my mouth and I can't speak, can't scream, can barely breathe. My wrists are still bound and he drags me along so fast I stumble to keep up. I know if I fall, it'll hurt the baby. I have to keep going. I have to be strong. For Lara. For Iris. And for my unborn child.

The back door whizzes open and the cool night air hits me in the face. It's fresh and clear, a welcome respite from the filth of the cage, but if we're on the move again, that will make me even harder to find.

My heart does that glowing thing again, and I swear I can hear his voice in my mind.

"I'm coming, Janie. I'm coming."

I hope so. I really hope so…

The strange alien insects which are just like Earth's crickets clack and buzz and click against the bracing night air. Grass, brambles, and twigs prick at my ankles and sting every bit of exposed skin. With every step, we're getting farther and farther away from Iris, Lara, and Isabella — and from safety.

But who am I kidding? It wasn't safe back there. It isn't safe here. And it won't be safe wherever I end up.

I can't hope to take Kovarx in a physical fight, but maybe if I could get my hands free, I could run…

A guttural roar cuts through the night and the birds sleeping in the trees scatter, cawing and crying out their displeasure. I'm rooted to the spot, and even Kovarx's frozen in place, looking for the source of the sound.

And there, among the shadowed silhouettes of the branches, a pair of glowing eyes pierces the darkness.

Eyes I'd recognize anywhere.

It's him.

Rathgar.

My Alpha.

HE LEAPS down from the trees and lands like a cat, his eyes still shining with murderous rage, fixed on Kovarx himself. I don't know whether to scream or cry or call out to him. I can't run to him. Not yet. Kovarx is still in the way.

"You're quicker than I thought, I'll give you that." Kovarx spits on the ground, lip curling. "But you're too late. I intend to take your woman with me as a replacement for the one you stole. And the others? The compound's set to self-destruct any minute now."

My heart jumps into my throat as I remember the looming countdown. Oh god! What if Lara and Iris and Isabella couldn't get out in time?

"Too late," Rathgar says. "We've already evacuated them."

A breath whooshes out of me. There's that, at least. But there's still the matter of my life on the line. And the life of my baby.

“You think you’re so smart. So noble.” Kovarx sneers at Rathgar, even as he’s advancing on him. “You act like your way is the only way — you’re just trying to oppress those who are different from you!”

With a growl that shakes the whole forest, Rathgar closes the distance between him and Kovarx, grabbing the alien around the throat with his wide hand and lifting him up into the air. Kovarx gags and struggles, clawing at Rathgar’s hand, but he’s too weak to make a difference.

“There’s one *very* different thing about you and I,” Rathgar snarls, looking right into his eyes. “And let this be the last thing you remember before you die: I do not use living souls as bargaining chips. I, and all the people under Soren's banner, seek to unify, not to isolate. And if you can't feel one ounce of regret, one iota of sorrow, well…there's only one solution. I tried to be merciful, but I've let this go too long."

I watch in horror, transfixed by the quarrel in front of me. This is a side of Rathgar that I have never seen before. I have heard stories, sure, and I always knew that the Aesirheim Alphas were practically genetically engineered killing machines, but seeing it so up close and personal like this…

Was it terrifying? Yes. But I would be lying if I said that some part of his steadfast determination and raw presence didn't make me hot in all the wrong ways.

"Y-you bastard." Kovarx squeaks out from his near-crushed windpipe.

"Shut. The fuck. Up." And with that, he drops Kovarx unceremoniously, letting him fall right onto the exposed blade of his sword. There's a gurgled cry as the bloody blade pierces through his body and comes out the other end, and then nothing.

Silence.

PROPOSAL

RATHGAR

It was over. Finally over.

I look at Kovarx's limp, bloody form on the forest floor. He didn't even deserve that quick of a death — I had intended to draw it out, make it hurt — but Janie was standing there, staring at me in horror.

Oh gods, Janie…

She probably thinks I'm a monster. She probably thinks that all that time I spent trying to be a good man and a good mate was wasted, if I can still spill blood so savagely.

The two parts of my life dance and intertwine, each vying for dominance. But as the two strands work their way together into a tighter bond, I realize that I don't have to give up one for the other.

My heart's pounding a mile a minute. Adrenaline and bloodlust still roars in my ears and pricks at my skin. The combined triumph of defeating Kovarx at last with finally rescuing Janie has me feeling a whole different kind of lust.

I step toward her, tentatively, still covered in blood. I know she doesn't want to see me like this, but…

Wait, she's throwing herself at me? Soft, human arms wrap themselves around my body and her head's pressed against my chest, the soft curls of her hair tickling my skin. Her body shakes with sobs and she clings on to me so tightly, afraid to let go.

"They've got—" she sobs between hiccups. "Lara and Iris, and Isabella too, we have to…" She points back in the direction of the compound. Right on cue, the building detonates, sending a fireball of debris and ash outward in all directions. Janie makes a broken wail. Her knees buckle, but I'm there to hold her up.

She didn't think…

"Janie!" I say with a bit more force than I intend. "It's all right. Soren and the other guys got them out of there. They'll be waiting on the ship for us right now."

She sniffs, looking up at me through tear streaked eyes. "Are you sure? What if they didn't get far enough away in time?"

"I'm sure."

"But what if…" Her chest heaves and her breaths come in quick succession. Must be the panic and stress catching up with her. I don't know much about emotions and even less about human emotions, but this can't be good for the baby. Soren and the gang are probably still busy, but…

My comm unit buzzes while I ping Soren. I don't expect him to pick up, but Janie needs proof from someone other than me.

"What's your status?" Soren's clipped, formal voice crackles through the tiny speaker.

"Target eliminated." Man, it feels good to say that. "I've got Janie. How about you all? You all right?"

"All accounted for."

"Is Lara there? Is Iris okay?" Janie speaks up. "We just saw the compound, and I thought..."

"Don't worry," Soren says. "They're here. They're fine."

Janie's still frowning, but I know she trusts Soren. We will all be together again soon. But in the meantime…

"See you back at the ship?" Soren asks. "Or you taking your own way back?" There's a subtle hint of something mischievous on top of his usual formality.

"We'll be along later," I say, schooling my expression to give nothing away. My heart's still racing, but this time it's for a totally different reason. If we hadn't arrived in time, I could have lost Janie forever. Iris, Lara, all of them…

I couldn't deny my feelings any longer. "There's something I need to take care of," I tell Soren. "We'll regroup with you all as soon as possible."

“Over.”

With a beep, the call ends. When I turn my head, Janie’s got her eyebrows raised in question. “What is this you ‘needed to take care of’?”

“This.” And with a grunt, I pull my omega against me, crashing my lips against hers.

It’s so fervent, almost animalistic in its intensity. I groan into her mouth and pull her ever closer, fingers running through her hair as she links her arms around me. I’ve missed this so much. And now she's here in front of me, all soft touches and warm smiles and the proud swell of her belly pressing against me. It's a constant reminder of our connection to one another, proof that one day soon, I'll be a father.

But no, that's not quite true either, is it?

I already am a father. Maybe not to my own, biological child, but I love Iris just as much as one of my own. She's wiggled her way into my heart, and there's no way I'm letting her — or her mother — go.

Finally, I break the kiss and look into her eyes. The fear's all gone now, and all that's left is a warm, steady affection that lights me up from the inside out. "I love you, Janie." I say. "I can't imagine my life without you." I pause. I've never been good with words. In the end, I go with my heart. "I know I'm not the best man or the best alpha, but you and Iris are my world. I dedicated myself once to my planet, and now I'd like to make a promise to you all over again." With a deep breath, I get down on one knee and look up at her. "Janie, will you be my wife?"

Her face is frozen in shock, and I don't blame her. It's not exactly the most traditional proposal. I mean, I've still got blood on my clothes, and there's a body lying a few meters away.

But somehow? It feels right. My heart thuds in time with hers, and there's no longer any doubt in my mind. My Janie is my heart-mate. Now and forever.

Her beautiful face breaks into a smile, and she buries herself in my arms all over again. "Yes," She says through choked-back tears. "Yes!"

"Good," I mumble against her hair. I'm kissing every bit of skin I can reach.

She's laughing, squirming, and smiling and I want to remember this moment forever. "Cause there's one more thing I need to do."

"And what's that?" She asks, already breathless from my kiss. And we're just getting started.

"Time to seal the deal." And I lower her to the ground with a triumphant, adrenaline-fueled passion that rivals even her heat cycle. There are no hormones or shots or serums to blame our feelings on this time. This is all us, all real. And I can't stand being apart from her a minute longer.

She's alive, the baby's safe, and our enemy is gone. Laying in a pool of his own blood just feet from where we're fucking. It feels so wrong, so dirty, but the bloodlust, relief, love, and pure carnal need makes for an intoxicating cocktail.

Janie responds to me just as fiercely, if not more so. She even uses her teeth to pull at my bottom lip, hands and soft nails digging into my flesh to beg for more, more, more.

And of course, I'm happy to oblige.

It's not the most graceful of couplings. Nor is it the most tender or the longest lasting. It's fast, hard, and frantic with endless streams of IloveyouIloveyouIloveyou punctuated by moans and thrusts and panted breaths. We're both so glad to see each other, so glad this is over, we pour all our frustration and fear and rage into the act, and when I howl out my release, I don't care if the whole damn galaxy hears us.

I'm making love to my omega, my wife-to-be, and no one is going to take her away from me ever again.

Mentally, I swear to her that we'll build our own happy ending.

CUTTING FRUIT

JANIE

I jerk awake, flashes of the raid still fresh in my mind. But my half-asleep mind is soon at ease when I see Rathgar slipping out of bed with a sleepy Iris.

"What's the matter?" I mumble, rubbing my eyes. It's not even light out yet. What are they doing up?

"Don't worry about it," Rathgar promises me. He leans down to press a kiss to my forehead and tuck an errant strand of hair behind my ear. "Get some sleep."

"But…" I feel like all I've been doing is sleeping, but Rathgar and the doctors say that's natural. My belly — no, my whole body — feels like an overinflated balloon, and if I don't have this baby soon, I might pop.

I want to get up, to help them with whatever they're doing, but my body has other ideas. Everything feels so heavy, and moving is about as easy as trudging through quicksand. I know he's looking out for me, but I don't like sitting around doing nothing. Never have.

But as I pull the blanket a little closer around me and snuggle further into my nest, maybe this time can be an exception.

VAGUE, varied thoughts float through my half-conscious mind. Am I dreaming, or am I simply thinking? I don't know. Thoughts and connections come and go like leaves down a stream.

Fire flickering outside the window. Shouts and footsteps. Splintering wood.

Iris crying in my arms. The damp cell

Rathgar, chasing us through the forest.

Kovarx's dead body, still impaled on Rathgar's sword as we screw like animals.

And Iris, sweet, sweet, Iris, calling Rathgar 'Dada' for the first time.

Despite what he thinks, Rathgar's really a better father than he gives himself credit for. He's caring and gentle where it counts, and the love he's shown both me and my daughter have changed my life. I thought I could never trust a man again after the incident with Iris's father.

But then again, Rathgar's not *just* a man. He's an alien, and an alpha, a warlord of Aesirheim.

And my husband-to-be.

I still can't believe he proposed to me in the heat of the moment with a dead body right next to us. It's crazy when I think about it, but somehow? It suited him. Suited us. And maybe I was possessed with the same crazy, because not only did I say yes, we went at it like beasts until we were both covered in sweat and dirt, as well as our enemies' blood.

There's no way I'm going to be able to sleep like this, so with a huff I pull aside the covers and carefully get out of bed. My back hurts. My feet hurt. My breasts hurt. When am I supposed to give birth again? It can't be long now, right?

Soft fur slippers rest beside the bed; I slip my feet into them, grateful for their warmth. Rathgar felled a creature on one of his hunts and used the pelt to make a blanket for Iris, among other things. The slippers remind me that even though Rathgar is a cinnamon roll when it comes to Iris, he's still a skilled warrior and an excellent hunter.

Throwing a shawl over my shoulders, I pad my way into the kitchen to see the rest of my family.

The word strikes a chord in my heart the way it never has before. *Family*. I had it with Lara, I had it with Iris, and now I have even more. With Rathgar and our upcoming child.

I stand there in the doorway for a moment, just watching them. I don't think they even notice I'm here yet, so absorbed they are in their task.

The sun just barely rises outside the kitchen window. The sky's a brilliant golden hue the same color as Rathgar's skin.

In the gathering light of the kitchen, Rathgar and Iris sit at the table with a bowl of fruits by their side. Soft melon. Bananas. Grapes. There are also several cookie cutters in all different shapes such as flowers, hearts, and diamonds. Iris holds a plastic knife and follows Rathgar's lead. His huge golden hands guide her own, pointing out each color and shape.

Educational *and* delicious. Smart.

I stay there for a second longer before revealing myself, just reveling in the warmth of affection that has grown in my heart. When I first met Rathgar, I thought he was a boisterous, grumpy alpha who didn't like anyone.

And while he can still have a surly personality at times, I've peeled back the layers to find the man underneath. Beneath the bravado and the muscles lies a loyal, steadfast lover who simply wants to make me happy.

Not just me, either. He took Iris in as if she were his own kin, and I have no doubt that he will be just as wonderful a father to our next child.

A soft thud in my lower belly reminds me just how pregnant I am. Soon, Iris will have a new baby brother or sister. My life will get a lot busier, but I've raised a newborn once before. And this time I have more help.

I never thought I'd actually find a man who I could trust again. I never thought I'd fall in love again, period. When I signed up for the ISA, it was simply something I had to do for the sake of my family. Now, I thank my lucky stars that it brought us together.

I let that warm feeling float through my heart and flow outward, until I'm practically glowing with it.

Iris looks up and catches my eye, hands covered in fruit juice. She waves brightly, plastic knife still in hand. "Hey Mommy!"

I step into the kitchen and join her at the table, looking at all the cute little shapes they cut out of the fruit. "Hey sweetheart," I say, kissing the top of her head. "Having fun?"

"Yeah," Iris says. "Oh! I made this one for you." She offers her closed fist and I hold out my hand. It's a piece of watermelon cut into the shape of a heart.

And here I thought my heart couldn't be any fuller.

"Hearts are for people you love. And I love my mommy."

"Thank you so much. I love it." And I wrap my arms around her, still unable to believe this is my life. From abandoned and pregnant the first time around to a house and a family full of love.

I look at Rathgar and he's resting his chin on his hand, eyes glazed over with the same sort of blissful peace mine are. "How long were you standing out there staring?" He says with a grin. "Thought you could sneak up on us, huh?"

I chuckle and wrap my arms around his neck. "What can I say? I'm happy. And you two looked so cute together."

Rathgar makes a mock pout, which is even more adorable given his gruff, scarred face. "I'm not cute."

"You are when you're with Iris."

He crosses his arms, but finally relents with a huff. He embraces me back and whispers in my ear. "You better not tell anyone else about that, though. I have a reputation, you know?"

"Whatever you say, you big teddy bear."

Rathgar snorts and shakes his head. "What am I going to do with you?"

An idea sparks to mind, and because he's sitting down I can actually reach. "Kiss me."

And as our lips seal together, we wordlessly promise one another a future. A family.

EPILOGUE

RATHGAR

"Dada, look!" Iris points into the water with the kind of pure, innocent wonder only a child can have. A long, red fish sweeps through the clear water and brushes against her leg, spouting up bubbles to the surface. "It tickles!"

"I think they like you — look, there's another one!" This time a pale white fish with golden stripes swims toward us. Seaweed and smaller fish float through the impossibly clear water, seemingly unperturbed by our presence. Ever since seeing fish at the lake nearby our house, Iris has been wanting to see them more up close.

Today's her birthday, and I promised I'd take her here, to the Crystal Sea, where fun and friendly fish swirl through the cool waters and colorful plants thrive both above and below water. It was a bit of a trek, but the look on her face makes it all worth it.

"Wooow!" Iris cries as one of the bigger fish flicks its tail and actually *jumps* out of the water for a split second. "Dada, did you see that? It's flying!"

I cross my arms and revel in the warm sun, watching Iris splash and play in the shallow waters. It's a perfect day for a refreshing swim, and the fact that it's Iris's birthday makes it all the more special.

"All right, you two!" Janie calls from back on shore. "Lunch is just about ready. Come in and dry off so you can eat."

"Aww," Iris groans, the cutest little pout on her face.

"We can play more after we eat, okay?" I take her hand and lead her back to shore. The feeling of her soft, small hand in mine is not lost on me. How did I get so lucky?

I never thought I'd find a mate. Never thought I was cut out for that kind of thing. But then Janie and her little girl crashed into my life — and into my heart. Every day with them is a blessing, and our new daughter Luna keeps us on our toes.

As we wade to shore, I see the little one on Janie's hip, breastfeeding while she reaches to keep the blanket from flying away in the wind. She's still so young, but already she's got fine, dark hair and her mother's eyes.

Iris runs to the blanket first, dripping everywhere. I grab a towel and throw it over her while I gather her up in a hug. "Gotcha!"

"Ahhh, Dada!" She screams, wriggling in my grasp. I ruffle the towel over her body and hair. When I've got most of the excess water off, she looks up at me with ruffled hair and a flushed, pink face. She says she wants to go play some more, but I know after she eats she's going to fall right asleep.

At least we've got a shady spot on the shore.

As I get her sat down on the blanket, Janie hands Luna to me while she pulls wrapped sandwiches and fruit out of a basket. I marvel at the idea — it's not so different from when my battle brothers and I have meals on field missions. That was out of necessity, though, and a lot less well-prepared than what Janie has for us.

"What was this called again?" I rub the back of my neck. I know I should remember, but I'm going to blame it on newborn brain. I knew that taking care of a baby would be a full time job, but I didn't realize just how much there was to do! Of course, we have Lara and Soren's help, but I'm not going to let my heart-mate raise this baby all on her own.

Not this time.

I pitch in wherever I can, whether it's changing diapers or looking after Luna so Janie can get some much-deserved rest. It's what she deserves.

"It's a picnic," Janie says with a smile. "You go to a pretty place and eat while looking at the scenery. It's fun."

Iris clearly agrees. "Mommy, the fish were sooo cool! You gotta go see them!" She's talking a mile a minute, and my heart swells with just how fast she's grown.

"After we eat," Janie promises, handing her a small sandwich she's cut into the shape of a heart and a juice box with a straw.

"Okay." The food keeps her quiet as we munch on our meals in pleasant silence. Overhead the calls of the birds greet us, and the sea breeze swirls through my girls' hair and laps at tiny waves on the shoreline.

I rest back on my elbows for a moment, just enjoying the feeling of being here together with them. For so long, my life revolved around battle. Around one mission after the next, never having a real purpose. Never having anyone — or anything — to come home to.

Now I had Janie, Iris, and Luna…and I'd be lying if I said I didn't want to see Janie full and round with another child again very soon.

Iris finishes her meal and, as expected, curls up in the corner of the blanket, blinking blearily up at us a few times before falling asleep. Janie puts Luna down next to her and I throw my arm around Janie's shoulders, bringing her close.

Our two girls. Beautiful, perfect girls.

I turn my head and give Janie a kiss. It's soft and sweet, nothing like the animal passion we shared during her heat. It's a kiss of contentment. Of peace.

"I hope you want a large family," I mutter as I tilt my head and press a kiss to her neck, then up to her ear. "Because I can't wait to fill you up again."

"Rathgar!" She squirms and laughs at my teasing, but her body melts against mine like it was made to be there. Her skin warms and tightens at my touch. "It's not even time for my heat yet—"

"That's okay," I cut her off with a kiss. Her cheeks. Her forehead. Her nose. Every part of my Janie is beautiful and deserves to be treasured. "We can still get some practice in."

Janie snorts and playfully pushes at my chest, but that just makes me grab her harder. We can't do anything out here with the kids so close, but my mind already spins with what I'm going to do to her once we get home.

"I love you, Janie." I say, holding her against my chest as we watch our sleeping girls. "Thank you for being my mate."

Janie snuggles closer to my body and lets out a sigh of contentment. "I love you too, Rathgar. Thank you…for helping me trust again."

"You deserve it," I remind her. "You deserve the whole galaxy, and more. You're mine now, and no one's ever gonna mess with you again."

As we gaze out over the Crystal Sea and the sun sinks lower on the horizon, I thank all the stars for my Janie and my family.

My very own miracle.

www.ingramcontent.com/pod-product-compliance
Lightning Source LLC
Chambersburg PA
CBHW030604310726
48979CB00003B/565

* 9 7 8 1 6 3 4 8 1 0 7 8 4 *